THE BENE'S DAUGHTER

A KI KHANGA ADVENTURE

....

MILTON J DAVIS

YOUNG LIONS PRESS

MVmedia, LLC
Fayetteville, GA

MVmedia, LLC
PO Box 143052
Fayetteville, GA 30214
www.mvmediaatl.com

Publisher's Note: This is a work of fiction. Names, characters, places, and incidents are a product of the author's imagination. Locales and public names are sometimes used for atmospheric purposes. Any resemblance to actual people, living or dead, or to businesses, companies, events, institutions, or locales is completely coincidental.

Book Layout ©2017 BookDesignTemplates.com

Ordering Information:
Quantity sales. Special discounts are available on quantity purchases by corporations, associations, and others. For details, contact the "Special Sales Department" at the address above.

The Bene's Daughter/Milton J. Davis. -- 1st ed.
ISBN 978-1-7372277-8-6

Contents

To Alana, Clarisse, Candace, Cammy, Ivy, and Alayna

Family is the strongest bond.

—Ki Khanga proverb

MILTON J DAVIS

"I am not a thief. I am not a thief." Omolewa repeated the words as she lurked in the dark alley between the compound walls, her eyes focused on the harbor across the walkway. A massive dhow rested among its smaller merchant brethren, a beauty of a vessel with clean white sails and a towering crow's nest peering down on the humble harbor. Why it had come to their modest Kiswala mooring of Nacala rather than the much larger harbor of Baseemah was a mystery. Omolewa did not dwell on the possible reasons; she cursed the consequences. She waited for a stranger that carried the key to her family's freedom, a scroll that once in the hands of those who held them hostage would end her family's terror and bring her life back to normal. At least she hoped it would.

Pik-Pik clawed her shoulder as she chattered into her ear, the ferret as nervous as she.

"Calm down!" she whispered. "You'll give us away."

Omolewa sunk deeper into the shadows. Hiding reminded her of the games she played with her friends when she was younger, but this was far from a game. The men who held her family hostage made that clear. They came to her family because of the rumors, the whisperings that Omolewa was not a normal child. Her ebony skin stood out in contrast to the average Kiswali soft brown tones, identifying her as a child from the hinterlands. Then there was the strange pattern that filled her forehead, an oddity she explained as a birthmark but a symbol that was much more. Some said she was a child of Eda, others a servant of Daarila. Omolewa felt what she now faced was her fault. She had not been discreet with her gift as mama and baba warned her to be. Now she and her family were paying the price.

"Bring us the scroll or they all die," the leader of the ruffians threatened. His face stood out in her mind not only because of the missing eye, but because his skin was dark like hers. He was the first such person she'd come face to face with in her life, the first person she'd met that resembled her in any way. There was no doubt he'd arrived on the large clipper resting in the harbor, for it hailed from Zimbabwa, the land of the Blameless Ones, the home of people like her.

Omolewa wiped his foul visage from her mind as she focused on her task. She closed her eyes and slipped into her second sight. Pik-Pik went rigid and ceased chattering. She did not understand what affect her powers had on her pet, but she knew her skills were heightened by its presence. Her mark transformed, emitting a blue glow that complemented her hooded dress. She extended her special sight around the corners of her lair then above the people traversing the road. She sought a man like herself, dressed in fine leather carrying a gilded satchel over his shoulder. He possessed what the ruffians sought. He was the key to saving her family.

She found the man they described strolling among the throng, ignoring the admiring looks and whispers of Kiswala folks. Omolewa changed her view of him, seeing him as if she faced him. He was handsome; deep brown flawless skin with a broad nose and captivating amber eyes. A thin mustache graced his full lips, joining with the tuft of hair on his chin. The way he stared made her think he could see her; the slight smile that came to his lips startled her. Did he know he was being watched? She pulled away. Of course, he didn't. How could he?

She readied herself as he neared the alleyway. She extended her right hand as focused on his satchel then moved her fingers. The satchel unbuckled and the flap lifted as he passed the alleyway. The scroll rose from the satchel and sped to her left hand. She snatched it from the air then shoved it into her dress pocket.

"Okay Pik-Pik," she said. "It's time to go home."

She hurried to the other end of the alley and melded into the market crowd. Not that she could meld. Omolewa was well aware of her story. Her father, a former Mikijen, discovered her abandoned as a baby on a campaign in Zimbabwa. Kiswala allied itself with the Blameless Ones against a threat from the Haiset, sending in their elite mercenaries to protect Kiswala interests. Baba found her in a village that had been overrun by Haisetti hordes and, captivated by her strength, hired a wet nurse for her with his meager earnings. After the war he brought her back to Kiswala. Mama readily accepted her; she was a Blameless One and nothing but good fortune would come to them with her as part of their family. Up until this day, good fortune had been their lot.

Omolewa worked her way toward the Backwater, the tattered working district where she lived. The family survived off baba's paltry pension and occasional carpenter's work. Mama picked up work when she could, weaving cloth and mending clothes. They were not wealthy, yet they were happy. Her nerves frayed as she approached her home, her eyes darting about to see if she had been seen or followed. Pik-Pik chattered and dashed from shoulder to shoulder, her restlessness reflecting Omolewa's mood.

She tensed as she reached plain wooden door to her family's home. She knocked twice as the one-eyed man instructed her to do. The door cracked opened, revealing his vile face. He snatched the door open, grabbed her wrist and dragged her inside. She ignored his brutality, her desperate eyes scanning the main room of the house. Mama and baba sat at the meal table, hands and legs bound and mouths gagged. Her siblings were crowded in a corner at the rear of the one room house, bound and gagged as well. Two men stood beside her parents, daggers in their hands.

The one-eyed man gripped her chin, turning her face to his.

"Where is it?" he asked.

Omolewa took the scroll from her pocket and handed it to him.

"Here. Now let them go," she said.

The man grinned as he placed the scroll in his shoulder pouch.

"A change of plans, darling. You're coming with us."

He looked at his henchmen. "Kill them all."

"No!" she screamed.

Pik-Pik leaped from her shoulders, landing on the one-eyed man's face. She sank her teeth into his nose.

"Aahhh!"

The man let go of her wrist. He stumbled away, pulling at Pik-Pik. The others laughed, giving Omolewa the time she needed. She thrust her hands toward the daggers at her parents' throats and they flew from the hooligans' hands. She jerked her hands back and thrust again. The men guarding her siblings winched and doubled over holding their stomachs. Omolewa tried to run to her parents but was jerked back, grimacing in pain as she fell on her back. The one-eyed man gripped her by her braids, his cheeks and nose bloodied.

"Don't make me hurt you, girl!" he shouted. "You're worth more alive than dead."

He dragged her toward the door. Omolewa tried to struggle but she was exhausted from her efforts. Tears streamed from her eyes as the men picked up their knives and returned to her parents.

"Finish them so we can go," the one-eyed man ordered.

A booming sound filled Omolewa's ears. She fell onto her back then watched incredulously as the one-eyed man sailed over her. A pair of boots appeared beside her, stopping briefly then proceeding in the direction of the table. She struggled upright and stared into the back of the man from whom she'd stolen the scroll. With the flick of his hands the men beside her parents flew left and right, each smashing into the walls with a crunching finality. He extended his hands and the men threatening her siblings flew into the air then slammed into the ceiling. He dropped his arms and they fell to the floor.

The one-eyed man lay before him. The man knelt to his side and grasped his face. He jerked the man's head and snapped his neck. The interloper stood and went to her parents.

Omolewa reached out with the last of her strength. The interloper slowed; he turned to her with a smile on his face.

"Don't hurt them, please," she begged.

"I won't," he replied.

He untied her parents then removed their gags.

"Eda bless you!" baba exclaimed. Both baba and mama ran to the back of the cabin to free her siblings. The interloper approached Omolewa and knelt before her.

"You are a terrible thief," he commented. "I followed you after you took my scroll. I'm glad I did. My name is "

He touched her and she felt a surge of strength.

He stood and stepped away. She was suddenly engulfed by her family, submerged by hugs and tears. Eventually they relented, allowing the mysterious man through. He carried Pik-Pik on his shoulder. Her furry familiar jumped from her perch and into Omolewa's arms.

"Thank you for saving us," she said.

The man nodded. "You've grown into a beautiful woman."

His statement made Omolewa curious and nervous.

"Do you know me?" she asked.

The interloper smiled. "I do, in a way."

Omolewa was perplexed. "How? I was brought here as a baby. That's what baba told me."

"That's what my baba told me, too," he said.

Omolewa looked to baba. He nodded.

"It's okay. I knew this day would come."

Omolewa turned to the man once again.

"I ask you again, sir. Who are you?"

The man knelt before her. " My name is Kulal Chihota, son of Bene Chadamunda. I'm your brother."

Omolewa stared blankly at the interloper. "Brother? I have only one brother, and that's Diwani. Baba told me my family was dead."

She looked at baba. "Tell him the truth, baba."

Baba looked away, his eyes downcast.

Omolewa's hands trembled. "Baba, tell him!"

"He told you what he was instructed to say," the man claiming to be her brother said. "Our homeland was not safe for you then. There were . . . forces that would have brought you harm if you were found, so you were sent here."

Omolewa's didn't want to believe what she was hearing. This man, apparently a powerful sonchai, claimed to be her brother. Baba knew him and had lied

14

to her about her origins. She was about to asked more questions when the room echoed with urgent knocking.

"Hello! Hello? Is everything alright in there?"

Baba went to the door and opened it. Three constables rushed in with short swords drawn. They looked at the bodies strewn on the floor then looked to baba.

"They attacked my family," baba said. "They wanted something from this man' — he pointed at the sonchai — 'and they forced my daughter to steal it."

The constables bowed to Kulal before examining the thugs. One of the constables knelt beside the body of the ringleader. He looked at the interloper expecting an explanation.

"He is of my homeland, but I am not familiar with him," Kulal said. "I will take care of his remains."

"I know these two," the constable said. "They're always causing trouble on the wharf."

The head constable joined the others. "Doesn't look like they'll do that anymore. Get them out of here."

The constables dragged the dead Kiswali outside.

"Are you sure you'll deal with this one?" the head constable asked. Kulal nodded his head.

"Then we will bid you farewell."

The constables left with their grim cargo.

Baba let out a breath. "That was too easy. They'll be back."

"Yes, they will," Kulal said. "But you will not be here when they return."

His words sounded ominous to Omolewa. Baba pulled her close.

"What are you talking about?" he said.

"My sister . . . your daughter must come with me. She is the reason I am here. It would be unrealistic for her to come alone. Although I am her blood family, you are her family in every other way. So, you must come as well."

Baba opened his mouth to answer but was interrupted by another door knock. This time Kulal opened it.

The man and woman entering Omolewa's home looked similar to Kulal; black skinned and handsome wearing robes that fell to the ankles of their studded leather boots. Kulal gestured with his head, and they went to the body of their nefarious brethren. A woman dug her fingers through the man's hair as if searching for something hidden. Her search stopped abruptly, and she looked up with a concerned expression.

Kulal knelt beside her as the woman pushed the hair away. Omolewa felt a sudden urge to see and broke away from her baba's grip. The man moved to block her way, but the interloper waved him off.

"She should see this. She needs to know her enemy."

Kulal gestured with his head and the woman moved aside. He pushed the hair aside, revealing a small curled horn on the side of the man's head. Omolewa's eyes went wide.

"Is that real?" she asked timidly.

"Yes, it is."

"Who . . . what is he?"

Kulal grimaced. "Joka Watu. From The Cleave."

Omolewa gasped. She waited for Kulal to tell her more, but he didn't. Instead, he stepped away from the body then pulled Omolewa aside. His brethren lifted the body then carried it away.

"You must come with us," he said. "I know this is sudden, but your lives are in danger, as you can see. We will be here for three more days. I will station my men around your house during that time but once we leave, we cannot insure your safety."

He placed his hand on Omolewa's shoulder and she felt comfort from his touch.

"You know I speak the truth, Omolewa," he said.

Omolewa grabbed his hand to remove it from her shoulder but held it instead. His touch made her feel safer than mama's embrace, but she was no fool.

"You are a sonchai, bwa," she replied. "I cannot be sure of anything around you."

Kulal smiled. "Very good sister but think on this. Your family is not safe if you stay. This is not their choice. It is yours."

Kulal smiled then exited. Omolewa and her family immediately converged, hugging and kissing and crying.

"You are safe!" mama exclaimed.

"We all are," her baba added.

Omolewa picked up Diwani and rubbed Kazija's head as she clung to her leg.

"You are a hero, Lewa!" her brother said.

Pik-Pik crawled from the corner then raised up on her hind legs next to Omolewa's leg. She reached down then picked her up.

"You brave little thing," she said.

Omolewa's joy was brief. The revelations of the past few moments settled on her mind.

"Baba," she said. "What is going on? Are Kulal's words true? Why did you not tell me these things?"

Mama took Diwani from her and pulled Kazija away as well. She looked at baba with the same questioning look. Omolewa realized that she was not the only person owed an explanation.

"I didn't tell you the truth, for I didn't know until the moment Kulal stepped through our door," baba confessed. "There are still things that are hazy."

The family sat around the table, looking at baba with a mix of expressions.

"How could you not know, Tayari?" mama asked.

"I promise you, Jamela, I did not know." Baba finally sat with them. "When Kulal walked into our home it was as if the sun emerged from behind a dark cloud. Images came to me that I knew was my true life."

"His . . . my family are people of ashé," Omolewa said. "They must have done this to you."

"Why would they do such a thing?" mama asked.

"To make sure Omolewa was safe," baba answered. "I could not share what I could not recall."

Baba closed his eyes for a moment then opened them. His expression was solemn as he looked at each of them, finally resting his eyes on Omolewa. The clarity in them confirmed the truth he was about to share.

"I was a Mikijen," he began. "A civil war raged in Zimbabwa, a war that threatened Kiswala interests in the region. I was the senior induna of my unit at the time. We received orders to march into the interior to protect a group of villages that supplied our dhows with yams and sorghum and secure the road leading to the coast."

"Did you fight for Kulal's family?" her brother asked.

Baba smiled. "No. Kiswala does not take sides in local conflicts. The Mikijen only protect Kiswala interests. We were marching into the valley when we came across a Zimbabwa army retreating from the north. To say they were in dire straits would be an understatement. We gave them food and tended their wounds. Their commander sought me out and asked for our help. They planned to return to battle, but of course we could not assist them. The commander understood, but then asked me to come with them. That's how I met you."

Baba's smile made Omolewa's cheeks warm. She smiled back.

"They took me to a man and woman whose clothing told me they were people of great importance. The man stood before the woman and extended his hands to her. She looked at him with worry then looked at me with sympathy. Then she handed him the child. He came to me directly."

"There is much turmoil in our land," he said. "Too much for our daughter to remain.

Zimbabwa has always been a volatile mix," I remember saying. "It will pass."

"There is a deeper evil afoot," he said. "One that comes from beyond our borders. We cannot take any chances."

"He gave you to me and said, 'Take my daughter with you. Her name is Omolewa. We will come for her when the time comes.,'"

I took you in my arms dumbfounded.

"I can't," I said.

The man's eyes took on a strange look, as if the storms of times resided in them.

"You can, and you will," he said.

Baba leaned back in his chair. "From that moment I believed the story I told you and your mama. He must have cast some type of spell on me. If I did not know the truth, I could not tell it if the wrong people found me."

Baba reached toward Omolewa and she fell into his comforting arms. She snuggled close to him, wishing she could stay this close to him forever.

"Today has been a trying day for us all, but for you especially," he said. "A great burden has been revealed to you."

"It's not fair," she said. "I did not ask for this."

"No one asks for the life they are given," baba replied. "We open our eyes, and it is there. All we can do is live it in the best way."

"Enough of this," mama interjected. "You can't make any decisions on an empty stomach. I'll make us stew and we will talk of this later. We have been through enough this day."

Mama sent everyone into a whirlwind of chores, trying her best to get everything back to normal. Omolewa was grateful for the distraction, but she couldn't forget for one moment the decision looming in her immediate future. She didn't want to go anywhere. Nacala was her home despite what this man claiming to be her brother claimed. A journey to Zimbabwa would be a journey to a foreign land. But the man said her decision would save many lives, and after what occurred she knew her life and that of her family were in danger.

They did not talk again of the incident and of her decision for there was nothing to discuss. As Omolewa prepared her siblings and then herself for bed she caught glimpses of baba and mama packing clothes and other items in a pair of wooden chests that served as tables. So they were going. That night as she lay in her bed, she stroked Pik Pik's soft fur and thought of this new adventure about to take place in her life.

- 2 -

Omolewa woke to pounding on their door; an image of the ruffians who held her family captive the day before flooding her mind. She searched about for something to defend herself. She would not be taken unaware this time. Baba rose from the bed and went to the door.

"Baba, no!" Omolewa shouted.

Baba looked at her and smiled, his eyes confident and assured.

"It's okay, Lewa," he whispered.

Baba opened the door, revealing Kulal's smiling visage.

"Good morning!" he said. "I pray I'm not too early."

"No," baba replied. "This is a late morning for us. We're usually awake but everyone needed a bit more rest after yesterday."

Kulal nodded. "I understand. May I come in?"

Baba stepped aside and her newfound brother entered. He walked directly to her and knelt.

"Good morning, sister."

"Don't call me that," Omolewa replied. "It doesn't feel right . . . yet."

Kulal's eyes revealed his disappointment, but he smiled regardless.

"It is a strange thing for me to say as well, but I decided the sooner I began the faster I'd get used to it.

Which leads me to the reason I am here. What have you decided?"

"We are coming with you," baba said.

"Excellent!" Kulal said. "I took the liberty of assuming you would. My people are coming for your things. Do you have any outstanding debts?"

Baba seemed surprised at Kulal's question.

"If a person breathes, they had debts," he replied.

"Make me a list of whom you owe and where they are located," Kulal instructed. "We will settle them immediately."

Baba's eyes bulged. "You will do this for us?"

Kulal looked at Omolewa. "You are family."

Baba turned to mama. "Jamela did you hear?"

Jamela sat upright in the bed, tears welling in her eyes. "Yes, I did."

She rushed by baba and hugged Kulal

"Thank you! You were sent by Eda, you were!"

Kulal hugged her back. "Save your joy. You may think otherwise later."

Omolewa's reservations diminished seeing the delight in her parents' faces. Kulal seemed a very good person. The feeling of future dread did not leave her completely, but she knew that whatever lay ahead Kulal would be steadfast.

Kulal's companions entered and gathered their belongings while the family awoke and dressed. The workers carried their baggage to a large wagon waiting in front of their home. A crowd gathered as the wagon was loaded, curious neighbors and passersby looking enviously at the apparent good fortune that had fallen on her family. As she looked into the eyes of strangers, she realized how few friends they really had. Another revelation came to her which filled her with guilt. Her father had deliberately distanced them from everyone to keep her secret. Except for mama's family, they had no friends. With Omolewa the isolation extended to her friendships. She had few. Her beauty was as ostracizing as it was attractive.

Kulal led them to a noble's coach hitched to six horses draped in gold stitching and cowrie trimmed finery. A warrior opened the door.

"You will ride with me," Kulal said.

Her brother and sister needed no urging; they giggled as they raced to the coach and clambered inside. Omolewa walked slowly with her parents in wonder.

"This is too much,' her mother whispered. "Too much."

"It's like a dream come true," baba added.

Kulal shook his head as he accompanied them. "If Omolewa lives up to her potential there will never be enough to thank you."

The word 'if' fell on her shoulders like a sack of sorghum. She searched her brother's smiling face and discovered another emotion lurking behind his visage; hope.

Their procession raised a stir throughout the town. By the time they reached the docks an enormous crowd had gathered, ululations rising and scarves waving. When Omolewa and her family emerged from Kulal's coach the crowd roared in approval. The family walked single file behind the Zimbabwa noble, waving like dignitaries. Omolewa's brother and sister were especially enthusiastic, blowing kisses as well. Omolewa tried to smile but it would not come. Her life would change forever once she set foot on the long black dhow with the towering sails, a dhow that would take her to a home she'd never known. As she scanned the vessel from bow to stern, a person caught her eye. He stood by the central mast draped in a white robe accented with golden thread about the raised collar. His skin was a darker brown than the Kiswala, but not as deep as the

Zimbabwans scurrying about the deck preparing to set sail. A golden cap rimmed by cowries fit snug on his head. His white eyebrows matched his short white beard; there was no other hair on his aged face. He stared at her with eyes that reflected intelligence, wisdom . . . and ashé.

Omolewa tugged on Kulal's shirt.

"What is it, sister?" he asked.

"Who is he?" she said, nodding her head toward the mysterious man.

Kulal grinned. "He will introduce himself soon enough."

She looked at the man and he smiled. Omolewa looked away, embarrassed.

As they proceeded up the gangplank the man approached them. Kulal greeted him with a respectful bow. The man returned the bow them came directly to Omolewa. Her baba hurried to her side.

"Who are you?" he asked. His voice was stern, but Omolewa detected fear in her baba's voice as well.

"I bear you daughter no harm, Tayari," he said. His voice was deep, resonant, and comforting.

"How do you know my name?" Baba asked.

"Who would not know the guardian of such a treasure," he replied. "Welcome to my dhow, Omolewa. I am Kashta."

Kashta extended his hand just as Kulal approached. Omolewa took his hand and was suddenly overcome by images. She saw an island split by a wide river, desert north of the waterway, forest to the south. She saw proud brown people living in towering stone homes and who practiced ashé and other mysterious skills. Her mental vision finally focused on a boy, a bright child whose life sped across her mind until she stared into the face of a man. It took a moment before she realized the face she gazed upon was before her and not in her mind.

"Now you know me as well," he said.

"Yes, I do," Omolewa replied.

Kashta turned to Kulal. "Please take Lewa and her family to their cabins. We'll be leaving immediately."

Omolewa's eyes widened. "How did you know my little name?"

Kashta grinned. "I told you, we know each other very well now. As I shared with you, you shared with me."

Omolewa looked at her father and he shrugged. She looked back at Kashta as he marched across the deck shouting orders. He was correct when he said she felt as if she had known him all her life. He was the most fascinating person she'd ever met, and he was to be her teacher. The journey to Zimbabwa could not get under way fast enough.

They followed Kulal below deck to the stern. The narrow hallway ended at an ebonywood double door carved with patterns and shapes that were strange yet beautiful to Omolewa's eyes.

"Is this our room?" she asked.

"No, this is Teacher Kashta's cabin. Your cabin is here." He pointed to a gilded door to the left of Kashta's cabin. "My cabin is across the hall."

Baba opened the door to the cabin and mama gasped.

"This cabin is bigger that our home!" mama exclaimed.

Her family rushed into the room, but Omolewa didn't follow.

"I want to go back on deck," she said.

Baba looked at her from the sumptuous room. "You should see this!"

"I've never been on a dhow before, baba. I want to see the outside first."

Baba and mama looked at each other then back to Omolewa.

"I'm an old Mikijen," baba finally said. "I've seen enough of the sea. I would be at ease if Kulal joined you."

Mama nodded in agreement. Her brother and sister were oblivious to the conversation, their attention absorbed by their comfortable beds and big pillows.

"Thank you for trusting her with me," Kulal said. "Come, sister!"

He grabbed her hand and they hurried to the deck. Kashta stood at the helm, his hands clasped behind his back. He looked at the duo as if expecting them.

"You two look as if you grew up together," he commented.

Omolewa looked at Kulal and they smiled. The apprehension she felt toward him diminished with every moment. Kashta seemed like a favorite uncle, and the dhow's crew like friends. She couldn't explain what was happening, but she was happy to be surrounded by so many people that seem to have her interest at heart.

The anchor rose with a loud clatter as the mooring ropes were tossed onto the deck. The sails were lowered, and they immediately swelled with a strong wind. The helmsman, a broad shouldered Zimbabwan, steered the dhow into the open harbor and they cruised by the other dhows. People waved goodbye and children followed them as far as they could along the dock, yelling and laughing along the way. Omolewa looked overhead, watching the seagulls flying along with them. As the dhow entered open water she looked to stern, watching the only home she'd ever know diminish into the horizon.

Another muscled Zimbabwan came to Kashta.

"When do we raise the stacks?" he asked.

Kashta glanced to stern. "Not yet. We must be sure we're clear their field of vision."

The burly man walked away. Omolewa was not about to let this mystery slip away.

"What are stacks?" she asked.

"You'll see soon enough," Kashta assured her. "Meantime you should return below. Your family misses you."

Omolewa nodded then hurried back to the cabin. Baba and mama had calmed but her siblings were far from done. Baba looked almost relieved to see her.

"You have come back," he said.

"Yes baba. This is a wonderful vessel."

"That it is," baba replied. "I've spent much of my life sliding across slick decks. To call this lovely thing a dhow is an insult."

She was about to answer baba when a shrill whistle interrupted them. Omolewa hurried back to the deck just in time. The sails had been furled and stored away. The masts were bare; a situation that even she knew was not good. Kashta stood with the others, their eyes on two square boxes that she hadn't noticed earlier.

"Open them up!" Kashta shouted.

The crew pulled at a series of ropes and pulleys, lifting the thick wooden tops from the squares. Once the covers were clear Kashta shouted again.

"Raise the stacks!"

The dhow shuddered. Omolewa yelped then grabbed Kulal. He laughed.

"It will be over soon, and then you will see a Kamite wonder."

The dhow continued to vibrate as two wide metal tubes rose from the boxes. By the time they finished rising her parents and siblings were standing beside her.

"It can't be," baba whispered.

27

The deck trembled and a droning sound rose from below. Minutes later the tubes hummed, and white smoke belched from the tops. Baba ran to the stern then peered over the bulwark. Omolewa joined him. The water churned beside the boat with a slow rhythm that slowly increased. As it increased the dhow began to move forward; slowly at first, then faster and faster. Soon they were travelling faster than the wind.

"It's amazing!" baba shouted.

"No, it's ashé," Kashta replied, "a special type that is within the grasp of men."

He placed his hand on Omolewa's shoulder. "I will teach you this, and so much more."

"What is it?" she asked.

"It is a device that runs on steam. It is driving the dhow."

Omolewa beamed. "It's wonderful!"

Kulal laughed. "The Kamites possess many wonderful things. They have come to share with us all."

Omolewa's good mood dimmed. "Why?"

Kashta nodded. "That is a good question, Lewa."

He patted her shoulder and walked away without answering.

"Come on," Kulal said. She liked the way he said her little name. "Spend time with your family. Once we reach Zimbabwa your days will be occupied. You'll grow tired of Kashta's face."

"I don't think that's possible," Omolewa replied.

Kulal laughed. "Believe me, it is."

She went to mama and baba and hugged them both.

"This dhow is remarkable!" mama said.

"Yes, it is, but I feel everything will become more serious once we land in Zimbabwa," baba replied.

"I think you are right, baba," Omolewa said.

"Lewa! Come run with us!"

Diwani and Kazija grabbed her hands and tugged her away from her parents. And thus, they spent the next few days roaming the fast-moving dhow and exploring ever inch they were allowed to. Baba and mama spent their free time locked behind the cabin door, much to the frustration of her siblings but to the amusement of Omolewa. She was old enough to know what they were doing, and they were doing it much more than they had in months. She wouldn't be surprised if her next brother or sister would be born in Zimbabwa.

Her siblings finally tired of the new adventure, worn down by repetition and sea sickness. Omolewa seemed immune to the illness, walking the deck like a seasoned sailor. She rose early one morning, donning her clothes and sneaking out of the room. To her surprise she met Kulal and Kashta in the hall. Both men had serious looks on their faces; Kashta looked concerned, Kulal worried. Kashta looked into her eyes and his concern transferred to her.

"Follow me," he said.

The trio marched to the upper deck. The Zimbabwans went about their chores, but their faces were tight, their motions stiff. Omolewa noticed them glancing into the sky as if looking for something.

"Can you feel it?" Kulal whispered.

"Feel what?" Omolewa whispered back.

Kulal looked into the sky and Omolewa was puzzled. What was she missing?

She followed Kashta to the helm. He stood by the steersman, the chugging of the mysterious engine driving the dhow matching the rhythm of her heart. He circled, his eyes searching the far horizons. As he looked starboard, he stopped the pointed.

"There," he said. "They are following us."

Omolewa looked into the distance confused. She saw no other dhows on the horizon.

"You are looking in the wrong direction," Kashta said. "Look higher."

Omolewa jerked her head up. "Into the sky?"

Kashta nodded.

Omolewa and Kulal looked into the blue grey sky. She spied a speck floating high above the undulating sea.

"It is a cloud," she said instinctively. Kashta's looked told her she was wrong.

"Joka Watu!" Kulal exclaimed.

The deck exploded in activity. The sailors rushed to the wooden chests on the deck, extracting bows and lances. Some climbed up the masts, positioning themselves with crossbows and full quivers.

"Come with me," Kashta ordered. Omolewa and Kulal followed the Kamite below deck to his cabin. They were about to enter when her family stepped into the narrow passageway, her father's face more serious than she'd ever seen.

"Are we under attack?" he asked.

"Yes," Kashta replied.

"What can I do?"

"How are you with a bow?" Kashta asked.

Baba's eyes narrowed. "Better than average."

"Good. We can use you."

Baba grasped Omolewa's shoulders. "Stay below deck with your mother and siblings."

"No," Kashta said. "We need her on deck as well."

Baba frowned at the Kamite. "I know she had special abilities, but she's just a girl. Her eyes should not see what is about to take place."

"I cannot stop what is pursuing us without her," Kashta replied calmly. He then looked Omolewa.

"This why we came for you," he said. "I'm sorry you had to learn the truth so soon."

Omolewa looked at baba, then Kashta, then back to baba.

"What must I do?" she said.

Kashta opened the door to his cabin. Omolewa expected an opulent scene but was instead greeted by a sparse room with a simple bed, table and chair. The only other object in the room was a large ebony wood cabinet beside the bed. Kashta went directly to the cabinet and threw the doors open.

"Here," he said to Omolewa.

Kashta handed her a bow. She'd seen few weapons in her life; her father owned a sword and a few knives from his Mikijen days. The bow was heavy; it was strung with a material she didn't recognize.

"I don't know how to use this," she said.

"Today it doesn't matter," Kashta replied. "Consider this intense training."

Omolewa looked at baba and he smiled.

"Stay close to Kashta and me," he said. "You'll be fine."

Omolewa saw the worry in his eyes but nodded anyway.

"Come," Kashta said. "We must hurry."

They ran to the deck. The commotion that filled the deck when they went below had transformed into nervous stillness. The seamen stood along the bulwark, against the mast, or perched on the sails armed with lances, swords, and bows. All eyes gazed at the object in the sky which had grown from a speck to a discernible object. It flew almost like a bird, its appendages moving up and down but not as fluid as the birds she knew. There was something else as well, a long white trail of smoke rising from the rear of the object resembling a translucent tail. She looked at the smoke rising from the dhow's stack and immediately saw a connection.

"These are your people," she said to Kashta. "Why are they pursuing us?"

For the first time Omolewa saw anger flash across Kashta's face.

"They are not my people!" he snapped.

He closed his eyes briefly. When he opened them, he seemed to have regained his composure.

"As your brother said, they are the Joka Watu. Although we share knowledge, we discovered it by different means. They are the reason why I came for you."

"They mean us harm," Omolewa concluded.

"They mean Ki Khanga harm," Kashta replied.

Omolewa could not conceive her actions protecting the entire world, but she could understand the threat to her baba, mama, and her siblings. She would do whatever she could to prevent that from happening.

She lifted her bow. "I am ready."

The thing in the sky gained on them despite their speed. An eerie silence commanded the dhow; Omolewa stood between baba and Kashta, her trembling hands holding the bow.

"The trick is to use your ashé as well as your hands to pull back the bowstring," Kashta instructed. "Follow me."

Omolewa and Kulal followed the Kamite to the rear of the dhow.

"Raise your bows," he commanded.

Omolewa looked puzzled. "But I have no arrows!"

Kashta gave her his familiar smile. "Trust me. Raise your bows."

Omolewa peeked at Kulal, and he calmed her doubts with a brotherly nod. She raised her bow.

"Now pull back the bowstring with your hand and your mind," Kashta instructed.

Omolewa watched as Kashta and Kulal drew their bowstrings with ease. Omolewa imitated their moves. Her bowstring did not budge. It was too hard.

"I can't."

"You're not using your mind," Kashta commented. "Pull the string like you attacked the men who invaded your home."

Omolewa closed her eyes. The bowstring pulled easily, coming back to touch her cheek. She opened her eyes with disappointment.

"There still is no arrow," she said.

Kashta grinned. "There will be. Now focus on the Joka. Release on the count of three."

Omolewa nodded slightly as she struggled to keep her concentration.

"One . . . Two . . . Three!"

The bowstring twanged as she released it. She looked ahead and sighed. There was no arrow; neither were there arrows from Kashta and Kulal. She glanced at Kulal.

"Keep looking,' he said.

Halfway between the dhow and the Joka three bright, slim shafts appeared. They streaked fast toward the flying craft, emitting a shrill sound. The shafts separated; the center streaking directly at the joka, the shaft to the right veering slightly toward the 'wing' and the third wavering as it dropped toward the sea.

That's mine, Omolewa thought.

The center bolt, Kashta's arrow, smashed into the joka's head and it wavered. Kulal's arrow grazed the right wing and the joka slowed. Omolewa's arrow grazed the joka's bottom. The craft did not move.

The joka continued to gain on the dhow.

"Everyone seek cover, now!" Kashta yelled. Zimbabwans scrambled for shelter, some hiding behind boxes and barrels on deck while others ran below deck. Kashta pulled Omolewa down behind the bulwark.

"I missed," she said.

"Yes, you did," Kashta replied. "But you did very well. I didn't think you would be able to shoot it. You are turning out to be what we all imagined."

Kashta's words made her both proud and nervous. She didn't have long to think of her feelings. The Joka's shadow blanketed the deck, followed by the whistles of hundreds of bolts released from its underside. The bolts clattered against the deck, the rattling mixed with painful cries. One bolt struck the deck only a few inches from Omolewa. The bone white projectile seemed almost to glow. She reached out to touch it but Kashta grabbed her hand.

"No!" he barked.

He let go of her hand as he stood. The Joka was in front of them. It tilted to the left then began to turn.

"It's coming back," Kulal said

Kashta stood tall. "Everyone below deck now!"

There was no hesitation to his command. Omolewa found her father then gasped. A bolt protruded from his shoulder. Despite the wound he smiled when he saw her.

He glanced at the wound.

"Don't worry, Lewa. I'm a former Mikijen. I've suffered much worse and lived."

He grabbed her hand. "Come on; let's go below as the sonchai ordered. He seems to know this thing and what it might do."

Omolewa lingered on the deck as the massive joka wheeled about in the sky. Baharia rushed by her, seeking safety below deck. Kashta walked along the deck, following the joka's movements. Kulal followed him, his eyes darting between the joka and the deck.

She removed her father's hand. "No baba, I must stay with Kashta and Kulal."

Baba grasped her shoulder again. This time his grip was tighter.

"Lewa, come below."

"Baba, please let me go," she insisted. "I have to go to Kashta. I must learn."

Baba's lowered sagged and his grip loosened. "You are right. You must learn. But be careful and trust your feelings. Kashta is a learned man, but all people make mistakes."

Omolewa kissed baba's cheek, which seemed to ease his fear.

"I will baba."

She scampered across the littered deck to Kashta and Kulal, her bow tight in her hand.

"It's a fascinating machine," Kashta commented absently. "Steam powered mostly, but another source as well."

"Kipande?" Kulal asked.

Kashta nodded. "Probably. But how do they contain it without hurting themselves?"

"Or do they need to contain it?" Kulal asked

Omolewa had no idea what they were talking about.

Kashta's head snapped toward Kulal, and a proud smile split his face. "Very true. If their origin is where we suspect, kipande may be to them like blood is to us."

He shared his smile with Omolewa. "You do not understand of what we speak, but you will. It is essential that you do."

He turned his attention back to the joka then pointed at the rear of the machine.

"Can you see the smoke?" he asked.

Omolewa squinted. A thin trail of smoke emerged from the rear of the joka.

"I see it!" she exclaimed.

"That is our target. We'll wait until it passed then shoot at it. That is if we survive its next pass."

There was no emotion in Kashta's voice, but his words raised fear in Omolewa. These people meant to kill them. She knew this, but the weight of it finally settled on her young mind. She decided that she would not let them.

The joka had turned about and glided toward them from starboard.

"Come quickly," Kashta said. "We must hide."

The trio ducked under deck. Moments later there was a large whoosh immediately followed by intense heat.

"The dhow is on fire!" someone yelled.

"No, it's not," Kashta replied. He waited for a few moments then opened the hatch then stepped back on deck. Omolewa followed behind. The deck was wet, as if a sudden squall had spent itself over the dhow. Vapor rose like ghosts into the sails. The heat lingered.

"Steam," Kashta commented. "Hotter than boiling water. It would scald any person it touched but leave the dhow undamaged, as you can see."

Omolewa did not understand what happened, but she understood the joka would return. She did not want that to happen.

Once again Kashta seemed to read her thoughts.

"Come, this is our chance!" he shouted.

They ran starboard to the bulwark. Kashta raised his bow; Kulal and Omolewa did the same.

"Aim for the base of the columns!" he yelled.

Omolewa released her bowstring in time with her companions. The glowing bolts streaked toward the joka as it began to turn. Kashta and Kulal's bolts struck true. Smoke and steam erupted from the joka's rear, and it shuddered. Omolewa's bolt reached the thing a moment later. It struck nearby as the joka flanked. The joka boomed like thunder then a fireball rose from the rear. It fell flat onto the sea, breaking into sections. Omolewa spied people emerging from the wreckage as a cheer rose from the dhow.

"There were people inside it!" she exclaimed.

Kashta nodded.

Omolewa looked at her new mentor. "We must save them!"

"They stay where they are. If they are lucky Daarila will be merciful and end their lives quickly."

He looked at Omolewa. "It is more than they would do for us."

He took her bow. "You did well. Go and see to your family. I promise you I will explain everything soon."

Omolewa hesitated before giving the bow cack to Kashta. The sonchai and Kulal walked away, Kulal turning back to share a smile and a head nod. Omolewa was halfway to the hatch when mama, Diwani and Kazija emerged from below. They rushed to her then fell on her with hugs and kisses.

"Thank Eda you are alright!" mama exclaimed.

Omolewa melted into their affection. Was she okay? She wasn't so sure.

- 3 -

The dhow arrived in the Zimbabwa port three weeks after leaving Kiswala. Omolewa stood on deck with her family as they docked. Zimbabwa was a green land, with high verdant hills rising beyond the port city. There were other dhows docked nearby, vessels with columns replacing masts. They spewed the same smoke as their dhow and the joka. Her thoughts went back to the joka and the people they left behind in the sea. She shuddered then hugged herself.

Kashta approached them, wearing a wide smile complementing his elegant robes. Kulal was with him as always. Her newfound brother wore a loose green robe, a golden necklace and a cap studded with golden buttons.

"Welcome home, Omolewa," he said. "I know it is unfamiliar and strange to you, but you will soon see that this is where you belong."

She looked at the land then to her family surrounding her.

"Home is here with me," she said.

Kashta smiled. "You are wise beyond your years."

A disturbance on the dock drew their attention. A large green painted wagon approached, drawn by creatures Omolewa had never seen. They resembled horses, yet they were smaller, and their hind quarters were striped.

"Mama has sent for us," Kulal said.

Kulal strode to the gangplank, gesturing for everyone to follow. Everyone did except Kashta. Omolewa looked back at him with questioning eyes.

"I'll be along," he said. "There are things I must tend to."

She felt baba's hand on her shoulder.

"Come Lewa. He'll be fine."

Omolewa walked with her family to the awaiting carriage. She had no idea of the path that lay before her, but she knew if she was with family everything would be fine. At least that is what she hoped.

Kulal led Omolewa and her family to the wagon then opened the door. Diwani and Kazija broke away from her parents then clambered inside. When Omolewa, mama and baba reached the wagon then looked inside they were stunned. Diwani pressed his cheek against the cushioned seats while Kazija lay on her back on the other.

"It's so soft!" Diwani exclaimed.

Mama climbed inside then lifted Kazija off the seat.

"Make room, little one," she said with a smile.

There was plenty space for everyone, but Kulal did not enter.

"Will you not join us?" Baba asked.

"No," Kulal replied. "I will ride with the others. It's been a long time since I enjoyed riding a quaggat."

He closed the wagon door.

"It's a three-day journey to Mutapa," he said. "I hope you packed your patience."

Omolewa opened Pik-Pik's cage and the white ferret quickly climbed up her shirt to nuzzle against her neck. She seemed as excited as everyone as the wagon lurched forward and the journey to Mutapa began. Omolewa joined her siblings, peering out the wagon window at the passing landscape. Zimbabwa was a lush land; every inch of earth thick with vegetation. Bushes and shrubs crammed the spaces between towering trees with canopies fat with vines which made them seem like one continuous plant. The branches writhed with primates of various kinds; some no bigger than Pik-Pik and others as large as a healthy child. Colorful birds flittered about among the branches, their whistles and calls competing with the cries and chatter of the primates. The only spaces between the trees were those carved by the local folks, their round homes crowned with conical thatched roofs. Their walls consisted of local stone carved from the nearby granite mounds then plastered with clay which was painted with colors as vibrant as the surrounding flora.

Omolewa's enthusiasm was short-lived. The view became monotonous and the steady rocking of the wagon lulled her to sleep. She was abruptly awakened by a nip on her ear; when she opened her eyes Pik-Pik chattered. The wagon has stopped, and the others were gone. Omolewa looked out the carriage and saw the others sitting around a large mat in a small clearing. She climbed out the wagon then strolled over to join them, rubbing the drowsiness from her eyes. Mama looked at her and grinned.

"There's my sleepy head," she teased.

She kissed mama and baba.

"Why didn't you wake me?" she asked.

"You needed your rest."

Kulal joined them at the mat, carrying a large iron bowl. A savory aroma emanated from the bowl, causing Omolewa's mouth to water.

"What is this?" her baba said.

"Something to sooth your hunger and your soul," Kulal said.

A young servant dressed in a simple white smock passed out bowls and spoons to everyone. Afterward he dipped a large ladle into the pot then poured the stew into each bowl. Omolewa waited until everyone was served as was custom in her house before dipping her spoon into the stew and tasting it. The flavorful concoction tingled on her tongue and caused her eyes to widen.

"This is tasty!" she said.

"And spicy!" mama said.

Baba and her siblings said nothing. They were busy emptying their bowls into their mouths. Kulal chuckled.

"It's good to see you enjoy our food so far," he said. "When the stomach is pleased the soul will soon follow."

The amazing stew was followed with cups of water and mango juice. They rested a few moments longer before climbing back into the carriage and continuing their journey.

As night neared the forests gradually diminished, making way for patches of grass that eventually merged into vast open savanna disrupted by clumps of low trees and shrubs. Omolewa leaned out of the wagon window.

"Kulal!" she shouted.

Her brother guided his mount to the wagon.

"What is it, Lewa?" he asked. "Is everything well?"

"Yes," she replied. "What land is this?"

"This is Mashona," he said. "The land of our people. We are close to Mutapa, the Bene's city. We'll camp tonight and, in the morning, set out for the city."

"You say this is our land. What of the coast?"

"Mashona is our traditional home," he said. "The coast belonged to the Kiswala."

"Our people?" her brother said.

Kulal nodded. "Yes, your people. This is how your father came to be here."

"He's right," baba said. "The Mikijen protected all property claimed by the Kiswala. The port cities along the Zimbabwa coast were owned by them under a trade agreement with the Mashona. After the war, the Kiswala turned the cities over to the Mashona. They believed the risk was not worth the benefit."

"Tell me about the war," Omolewa asked.

The joy faded from Kulal's face.

"There will be time enough for that," he said. "Would you like to ride a quaggat?"

"Yes!" Omolewa exclaimed.

"Me, too!" Diwani said.

"Me, too! Kazija repeated.

"You'll get your chance, little ones," Kulal said. "This is not meant to be fun."

Omolewa looked puzzled. "It's not?"

Kulal looked at her seriously.

"No, it's not. This will be an introduction."

"It is that difficult?" Omolewa said as she looked into the beast's eyes. "It seems very calm."

"This is quaggat has been well trained," Kulal said. "As has all the quaggats on this expedition. You'll get your formal training once we arrive in Mutapa. We can't take any chances with you getting injured."

Kulal's last words made Omolewa uncomfortable. With the exception of their confrontation with the Joka Watu, Omolewa still couldn't cipher why she was important. She knew Kulal was a powerful sonchai, and Kashta's confidence could dull the sun. How was she expected to be a part of Kashta's plans?

Kulal rode up to the driver.

"Slow the wagon," he said.

The driver pulled back on the reins and the quaggats slowed their pace. Kulal looked back to Omolewa and nodded. She opened the door and mama grabbed her shoulder.

"Be careful now," mama warned.

"I will," Omolewa replied.

She climbed out of the slow-moving wagon. Kulal dismounted the quaggat then motioned to Omolewa.

"Turn your shoulders square then grabbed his mane," Kulal said. Omolewa did as instructed. The quaggat shuffled about, shaking his head.

"I don't think this is a good idea," she said.

"It's okay. He's just a little nervous. Now put your left food in the stirrup then bounce up with your right leg as you pull up with your left hand. Swing your leg over his back then put your foot in the stirrup."

Omolewa pulled the quaggat's mane as she bounced. The quaggat let out a high pitch squeal then bolted. Omolewa squealed as well as she fell on her back. Kulal was immediately by her side.

"Are you okay?" he asked.

"No," Omolewa said.

She stood then dusted off her clothes and baba ran to her.

"Lewa, are you hurt?"

"No," she said. She glared at Kulal, who was doing a bad job at holding back a laugh.

"We'll try again later," he said.

"No, we won't," Omolewa said. She stomped back to the carriage and climbed inside.

"That was funny," Diwani said.

"Shut up," Omolewa replied.

The caravan was only a few minutes out of the forest when night finally caught up with them. They reached the rest area as the sun carried away its last light below the horizon. They set up camp just beyond the tree line, the grasses illuminated under the light of an almost full moon. The night meal consisted of fruits and a type of sweets Kulal called mapopo. One bite and Omolewa knew not to eat anymore. One more bite and she would be addicted. After the meal they retired to their tents. Omolewa shared with her siblings while mama and baba had their own private tent. After camp was settled Omolewa could not sleep, and neither could Pik-Pik. She crept out of the tent, careful not to wake Diwani and Kazija. Someone else roamed outside of the tents as well. It was mama. Omolewa placed Pik-Pik in the grass.

"Go on now," she said. "You've never had this much room to play."

Omolewa made her way toward her mother. As she neared, she realized that mama was crying.

"Mama?" she said.

Mama jerked her head about, staring at Omolewa with tearful eyes. She tried to wipe her eyes with her blouse while smiling.

"What are you doing out here Lewa?"

"I couldn't sleep," she said.

"Neither could I," Mama replied.

Mama sat in the grass then patted the space beside her. Omolewa immediately trotted to her mother then sat beside her. She wrapped her arms around mama's waist and mama draped her arms around Omolewa's shoulders.

"Mama, why are you crying?"

Mama held her tighter. "You know me. I always cry."

"You cry for a reason," Omolewa replied. "Are you sad that we are not home?"

"I am," she said. "This is the first time I've been away from Nacala. I'm not the traveler your baba was. I like to know the ground under my feet."

"I don't think that is why you are crying, mama."

Omolewa felt mama pull away. She raised her head and found herself staring into mama's brown eyes.

"Is perception part of your talents too, young lady? We told you never to use your gifts on us."

"It's not my gift," Omolewa said. "Although I do feel them stronger here. They seem more natural. You're my mama. I know you, too."

Mama's eyes glistened. "That's because you are home."

Omolewa now knew why mama was crying.

"This is not home," she said as she lowered her head then pressed it against mama's chest. "Nacala is home. You and baba are home. And Diwani and Kazija are home when they behave."

Mama laughed. "Yes, it is."

A sharp squeal broke their mood. Omolewa was awash with a sudden sense of dread as Pik-Pik bounded from the darkness then leaped onto her shoulders. A large form lumbered toward them, a massive feline with a mane as black as the night. Two daggerlike fangs as protruded from each side of its large mouth. It resembled a shumba without a mane, but it was much larger. The beast stopped a few strides from them, its golden eyes locked on Omolewa. Omolewa fought her fear as she lifted her hands. She'd never faced such a thing; she was not sure her ashé was strong enough to stop it.

"AAAYYYEEE!"

A blur came from her right, striking the beast and knocking it from her vision. A warrior straddled the beast's back, his arms barely wrapping around its neck. The beast rolled over the warrior. Omolewa heard the man gasp as the beast came up on all four legs over him. It clamped its mouth over the man's neck then tossed him aside like a rag doll. The beast returned its focus to Omolewa then stalked toward her, mama and Pik-Pik. Omolewa's fear left her as the symbol on her forehead warmed. She felt Pik-Pik grip her neck, her softness re-assuring. She extended her arms, her palms facing the creature as she released her ashé as the beast sprang. Confusion flared in its eyes as it froze in mid-air inches away from Omolewa, caught in an unseen net. The beast struck at her with its paws, ripping with bared claws. Omolewa's arms shook, her head sweating from the heat emanating from her mark, but she would not yield. The beast stepped back, opened its maw and released a deafening roar that hit Omolewa like a physical blow. Her arms dropped and she stumbled back against mama.

"Lewa!" mama shouted.

Lewa looked at mama, attempting to hide her fear.

"Run mama," she said. "Now!"

"No!" Mama shouted back. "I will not leave you!"

The feline attacked now that her barrier had failed. Omolewa shielded mama with her body, bracing for the pain to come. More warriors sprinted to the fray but would not reach them in time. The shumba leaped toward them, its mouth wide and claws spread wide. Omolewa turned over to her back and raised her arms, digging deep inside to release the remnants of her ashé The shumba fell into the resurrected barrier, its bulk suspended over Omolewa, Mama and Pik-Pik. Omolewa's arms quaked; the shumba was too heavy. It slowly descended toward them, its jaws snapping.

A thunder like rumble battered her ears and the shumba disappeared. Omolewa dropped her arms as fatigue overwhelmed her. The warriors swarmed around them, shields and spears at the ready. Beyond them the shumba roared and a man shouted back. It was Kulal. She struggled to her feet then pushed through the warriors to see. Kulal stood wide-legged before the beast, shield and spear in hand. Kashta stood behind him, no weapons in sight. Kulal and the beast battled at an incredible speed, filling the air with curses, roars and blood. The beast emitted an eerie cry then staggered away from Kulal, its head jerking from side to side as if it sought escape. But Kulal would not be denied. He leaped at the beast, plunging his spear into the shumba just behind its right foreleg. The beast shuddered then fell onto its side, its bulk pulling the spear from Kulal's hand. He immediately drew his sword but there was no need for it. The beast let out a final roar then died.

Kulal's shoulders slumped as he turned away from the beast then trudged away. He bled from several places, but no wound seemed serious. Kashta patted him on his shoulder as he walked by the senior sonchai and Kulal shared a weak smile. His smile faded as his eyes settled on Omolewa. She felt his anger, as did Pik-Pik. She stepped away, hiding among the warriors then found mama's arms. She felt another hand on her back and knew it was baba. She looked into his disapproving face.

"What were you two doing out here alone?" he asked.

"Not now husband," mama said.

"Yes now," baba replied.

Kulal interrupted them. He stood before the family, his sword sheathed and his shield upon his back.

"You must never go anywhere alone until we are inside the walls of Mutapa," he said.

"No one told me this before," Omolewa said.

"It should have been obvious Lewa," Kulal fussed. "You are the Bene's daughter."

Omolewa's fear became anger.

"Do not call me that!" she said

"Call you what? The Bene's daughter? That is who you are," Kulal said.

"No. Do not call me Lewa. That is what my family calls me."

Kulal scowled then marched away.

"I want two warriors with her at all times," he said. "Never let her out of your sight."

"That was not nice Lewa," mama said. "He saved our lives."

Omolewa hugged mama. "I'm sorry. He made me angry."

The warriors parted as Kashta approached.

"Are you okay?" he asked, concern heavy in his voice.

"We are," mama answered. "Thank you."

Kashta nodded. "You must understand Kulal's mood. He was charged by the Bene to bring you home and protect you. He almost failed."

Omolewa glared at Kashta.

"You could have helped him fight that thing," she said. "Yet you did not."

"True," Kashta replied. "But rest assured I would not have let the shumba harm him. We learn from struggle. Kulal defeated the shumba and is stronger because of it. We will collect its teeth and hairballs. That was a powerful beast. Both will add to his ashé."

"Come," baba said. "Now is not the time for lessons. It's a time for rest."

Baba led them back to their tent where Diwani and Kazija waited. Their joyful naivety softened the mood as they family settled in for the rest of the night. But Omolewa couldn't sleep. Once again her life had been threatened by forces she did not understand. She was beginning to regret this so-called talent she possessed, and she was unsure of Kashta's motives. Pik-Pik chattered in her ear as she rustled about.

"You feel it too, don't you," she whispered. "We must be very careful. I'm not sure our friends are our friends."

She shared the rest of her food with Pik-Pik then tried to sleep.

- 4 -

Four days after the shumba attack the party arrived at Maputo. Omolewa looked upon the royal city in awe. Never had she seen such a magnificent place. Maputo sprawled among numerous hills and peaks, filling the valleys and in some places scaling the steep mountainsides. Wide avenues cut between rows of stone buildings of various heights; the streets vibrant with more people she thought could live in one place. Numerous waterways flowed throughout the city, some natural, some man-made, all spanned by sturdy, beautiful bridges. A thin mist obscured the tallest peaks. One hill rose over the center of the city, capped by what seemed to be a city within the city with tall towers rising even higher over the hills.

Kulal joined her, riding his quaggat. He was in a much better mood since his wounds had healed, but Omolewa was still reserved about him. She pulled closer to baba.

"Welcome to Maputo!" he said.

"It has been a long time since I've seen it," baba replied. "I've forgotten how magnificent it is."

Kulal pointed at the central hill.

"That is our destination," he said to Omolewa. "The Bene's palace."

Kulal reached into his pack then extracted a small horn then blew three short high-pitched notes. Two warriors rode up to him then nodded.

"Ride ahead and announce our arrival," he ordered. "We will wait until your return."

The warriors galloped away. Kulal smiled at them.

"I must go. We must prepare for our grand entrance."

"You are making quite a fuss about us," mama said. "Is this necessary?"

"Of course, it is," Kulal replied. "The Bene's daughter has finally come home. Our family is complete."

He rode away, shouting orders. The warriors formed ranks as servants took their spears and attached red rectangular banners to them. They lined two abreast, with Kulal and Kashta forming the vanguard. In the center of the procession was the wagon containing Omolewa and her family. The warriors Kulal sent out earlier returned, stopping to exchange words with Kulal then taking their place at the end of the column. Kulal rode down the ranks, hesitating at the wagon then winking at Omolewa and the others. He rode back to the lead on the opposite side. Once he reached the head of the column, he raised his horn and blew one sonorous note. He was answered by a chorus of horns and the rumble of drums.

The procession marched toward Maputo. Diwani and Kazija were beside themselves, bouncing from one side of the wagon cabin to the other, clapping their little hands in time with the vigorous drumming. Baba and mama nodded their heads in time until baba's eyes widened, and a smile came to his face.

"I remember!" he exclaimed. "I remember this song!"

He sang in a language Omolewa couldn't understand but his melodious voice conveyed the joy of the words. Mama hummed with him after a time; Diwani jumped into his lap and attempted to sing the words while Kazija continued to run and clap. Omolewa forced a smile to her face, petting Pik-Pik who was curled in her lap. She wanted to be happy, but the events of days ago still bothered her. It wasn't so much the shumba attack; the shock of it was slowly fading as she gradually accepted the purpose of her journey. No, what troubled her most was Kashta's response. The learned Kamite never promised her this duty would be easy, nor was she promised it would be safe. The encounter with the Joka Watu was the first indication. What worried her was how far the sonchai would go to make sure she learned what she needed to know. A knot formed in her stomach, and she lowered her head so her family would not see her grimace. Pik-Pik stirred. She climbed up to Omolewa's shoulders then snuggled against her neck.

"I know sweets," she whispered. "Do not think too far ahead to bridges you have not crossed. False worry is a burden you need not carry."

The processional entered Maputo. Omolewa's solemn mood could not deflect the energy and enthusiasm greeting them. The sidewalks undulated with the throng, each person singing the song baba sang in the coach. Drummers mixed with the spectators and filled the roofs of the lower buildings, swaying in time with their rhythm. As they reached the center of the city the song faded into a chant which caught Omolewa by surprise.

"Omolewa, Omolewa!'
"The daughter has come home.'
"Omolewa, Omolewa!"
"She's back among her own!"

Baba and mama looked at her with tears in their eyes. Diwani and Kazija came to sit beside her.

"You should wave at them," Kazija said.

"No, I don't think so," Omolewa replied.

"Let me show you!" Diwani said.

He leaned out the cabin window, waving with both hands. The crowd responded with roaring laughter. He pulled his head back in, grinning.

"See? Now you do it!"

Omolewa hesitated, looking at mama and baba for approval. Mama smiled then motioned her hand toward the window.

"Go ahead," she said.

Omolewa pulled the pulled the curtain aside then stuck her head out of the window. The crowd cheered, the drum cadence increasing as she waved to the throng. Kulal appeared, a wide smile on his face.

"Our people are happy that their princess has returned," he said.

Omolewa's smile weakened. "How can they be so joyous? They don't know me. This is the first time they've seen me."

"Not the first time," Kulal said. "You look just like our mother."

Hearing him say 'our mother' made Omolewa uncomfortable. She shared another wave then pulled away, closing the curtain. Mama and baba seem to sense the change in her mood. Mama reached across and placed her hand atop Omolewa's and baba smiled.

"It will be fine Lewa. You'll see," baba said. "So much is coming back to be now. It's as if a damn to a hidden part of my memory has been broken."

"I hope so," she replied.

"It will be, trust me."

Mama squeezed her hand. "Trust us."

The energy of the crowd never wavered as they proceeded through the city then up the spiraling road leading to their destination; as a matter of fact, it increased the closer they came to the Bene's palace. The procession slowed then came to a halt; Diwani and Kazija immediately took to the windows. Diwani pulled his head back in, grinning.

"We're here!" he said.

Omolewa pulled Diwani aside.

"Let me see."

Omolewa looked upon the palace, the home of the Bene. The walls were much higher than she'd imagined, consisting of granite stone from the nearby mountains. The surface was festooned with carvings of people and animals in various poses, depicting scenes of mundane daily chores to battles. Atop the wall were the largest drums she's ever seen. The men and woman drummers stood on platforms, holding their batons across their chests.

"Enter!" a female voice shouted.

The drummers played, the deep sound of the massive instruments rumbling against her stomach. Diwani and Kazija giggled has they held their stomachs; the feeling made Omolewa uncomfortable. Pik-Pik seemed annoyed as well.

She chattered and pulled at Omolewa's shirt with her claws. Omolewa stroked her fur.

"Calm down," she whispered. "It will be over soon, I hope."

The gilded gates of the Bene's palace swung open with an ease that belied their massive size. The drummers continued playing but at a lesser volume. The procession moved again, this time at a slower pace. Omolewa got up from her seat and sat between mama and baba who both draped their arms around her shoulder. Pik-Pik fussed as she scampered down to her lap. Diwani and Kazija crowded in as well.

"This is it," Omolewa said.

"Yes Lewa," mama replied. "This is it."

The procession passed through the gates of the Bene's palace, entering a wide courtyard filled with warriors dressed in leather and iron armor accented with gold. They fell to one knee as the carriage passed, their heads lowered. After the ranks of warriors were the palace servants. Men and women were dressed in silken tunics that exposed one shoulder and fell to just below their knees. The women sported elaborately braided hair; the men were bald. Some of the men and women wore gold bands around their left biceps and stood before the others. Omolewa assumed these were people of position, leaders who probably took direct orders from the Bene or other family members. Diwani and Kazija squeezed next to her, sticking their arms out of the carriage window and waving.

"Hi! Hi!" they shouted.

The servants laughed and waved back.

Three people stood before the palace entrance, each dressed in elaborate robes with golden helmets upon their heads. Kulal and Kashta rode up to the trio then dismounted; servants appeared immediately to take their quaggats. The columns split into single file, veering right and left and circling away from the palace to join the ranks of the other warriors. The carriage driver guided the wagon up to the others then brought it to a halt. Servants appeared at both sides of the wagon then opened the doors and placed step stools. Mama and baba exited the left door; Omolewa, Diwani and Kazija exited the right. The little ones lost their boldness once outside and clung to Omolewa's legs. Pik-Pik clung to her neck.

"Take my hands," Omolewa told her siblings.

"No!" they said in unison.

"I can't walk with you holding my legs," she replied.

Mama and baba appeared. Baba lifted Diwani into his arms and mama took Kazija. They walked together to Kulal, Kashta and the others who greeted them with warm smiles. Omolewa looked at the woman standing in the center, her eyes wide with wonder. She walked up to the woman then bowed.

"Hello…Bene," she said.

The woman laughed. "No child, I am not the Bene. I am Hajanika, the Bene's consul. The Bene sent me to greet you and your family. Welcome to Maputo."

Hajanika went to baba and shared a smile as well.

"Welcome back, Tayari. It is good to see you again."

Baba's brow furrowed as if he strained to remember the woman standing before him. One of the men stepped forward, his finger extended. He touched baba's forehead.

"Remember," he whispered.

Baba's eyes fluttered blankly for a moment. Recognition came to him and he smiled.

"It is good to see you as well, Hajanika. It has been a long time."

He looked at mama, wrapping his free arm around her.

"I remember now Jamela," he said. "I remember everything."

Hajanika shared a smile with mama.

"Jamela. A lovely name for a lovely woman."

Mama's smile was strained. "Thank you."

Hajanika stepped away.

"Please follow me," she said. "The Bene waits."

The entry guards grasped the golden handles of the palace doors then pulled them open. Hajanika strode into the palace followed by her companions. Kulal and Kashta came and stood by Omolewa and her family.

"Come," Kulal said. "We will walk together."

They crossed the threshold of the Bene's palace, entering a wide atrium filled with an array of flowering plants and fountains. Hummingbirds flittered about the blooms, while servants stood at attention. There were benches under some of the larger plants; one servant sat under a gathering of fronds as she read a pamphlet. She looked up to see the entourage passing through then jumped to her feet, an embarrassed smile on her face.

"That's Bukene," Kulal said. "She's always reading. Gets her in trouble all the time."

Omolewa frowned. "I can read Kiswala, nothing more."

"Kashta will teach you," Kulal said. "He will teach you many things."

"Did he teach you?" she asked.

"No," Kulal said. "I was tutored by Hajanika since I was a child. The Bene also provides education for the people of Zimbabwa. Education is very important to us. It is important to know of the world's wonders."

"Kiswala has schools," Omolewa said. "Mama and baba could not afford them."

Kulal nodded in understanding. "It is like that in many places in Ki Khanga. But not in Zimbabwa. Education is free to anyone that wishes it. The Bene believes it is essential that every person is educated to their highest level to truly exploit their talents."

Omolewa felt nervous when Kulal mentioned talents. She was about to respond when they exited the atrium and entered the corridor leading to the Bene's receiving room. The hall was almost as wide as the atrium. Twenty warriors could stand side by side with space between them and fit comfortably. Carpets from throughout Ki Khanga hung from gilded rods supported by chains from the ceiling, each one decorated with colors and patterns from their origins. Omolewa was impressed yet familiar with many designs, having worked at the Nacala docks and witnessing the variety of cargo passing through the Kiswala ports.

"That one is from Matamba," she heard Baba say to her brother and sister, "And that one is from Asanteman."

"Where's that one from?" Diwani asked, pointing his finger at a beautiful carpet that seemed to shift as if it possessed life.

Baba frowned. "That is from Fez. Do not stand too close. Their magic infects everything they create."

Diwani whimpered as he gripped Baba's neck tighter. Omolewa felt an odd sensation emanating from the fabric. Whatever it was, it was not ashé. Chills passed through her and Pik-Pik.

"I know what you feel," Kulal said. "The people of Fez have their own power."

"It feels...unnatural," Omolewa said. "I don't trust it."

"You do not trust us," Kulal said. "You see us as you see that carpet, exotic and strange."

Omolewa cut her eyes at her new found brother.

"A few weeks ago, I was living as normal a life as I could with the talents I possess," she said. "Then you appear and my life changes. I'm still not sure if it is for the better or worse."

"If we could have left you where you were, we would have," Kulal said. "But circumstances have been set in motion that will affect us all. We must be ready when they manifest themselves fully. You saw the Joka Watu; you saw the shumba. This is only the beginning."

"I should have been given a choice," Omolewa said.

"A choice to do what?" Kulal asked, anger in his voice. "Die with your family in Nacala? Times will soon be upon us where that will be the only choice, unless people like you, me and Kashta stand up to make a difference."

"That's enough," Kashta said. "You get ahead of yourself."

"She needs to know this is no game!" Kulal replied.

"I think she is already aware of that," Kashta said. "Which is why she is unsure. Am I right, Omolewa?"

Omolewa looked at the sage then nodded.

"I understand," he said. "Your mother will explain everything to you."

"My mother?"

Kashta smiled. "The Bene."

"You must learn to think of her that way," Kulal said.

"I have a mother," Omolewa replied. "I will decide if I need two."

At the end of the corridor were the doors to the Bene's receiving room. Like the doors to the palace two guards flanked them, but these guards wore no weapons. Both were women dressed in shirts with billowy sleeves and wide skirts. They smiled pleasantly as the entourage approached.

"Who are they?" Omolewa asked Kulal.

"The Bene's Flowers," Kulal replied. "Her personal bodyguards."

"They wear no weapons."

"They do not need them."

The women bowed, paying special attention to Omolewa. They opened the doors to the Bene's receiving room. One of the women smiled warmly then winked at Omolewa.

"Welcome home, sister," she whispered.

They entered the Bene's chamber. Omolewa expected a room filled with precious objects and fawning sycophants. Instead the Bene's receiving chamber was sparse. Cushion benches sat against curved walls decorated with simple nature paintings. At the opposite side of the room sat the Bene in a throne that was merely a large chair with a raised back. She was dressed in a simple green dress gathered about her narrow waist with a corded leather belt. Her hair extended from her head in a cone shape, decorated by strands of white beads and cowrie shells. As her face became more distinct Omolewa could see why everyone knew her. Though she had only seen her reflection a few times, this was the first time she'd seen herself in someone else's features. And then there was the telling sign, the faint pattern that graced her forehead, the same mark Omolewa possessed. The sense of place that spread throughout her made her feel a sense of betrayal. Her mama walked with her toward this regal woman, yet this woman sitting before her resembled her as mama and baba never could.

Pik-Pik jumped from her shoulders then ran toward the Bene.

"Pik-Pik no!" Omolewa shouted.

The weasel scampered up the Bene's dress then curled up on her waist. The Bene laughed, a cheerful sound that forced a smile on Omolewa's face. Their eyes met and the familiar feeling between them increased.

They reached the base of the Bene's dais. Everyone prostrated before her except Kulal, who hurried up the stairs then hugged the Bene tightly.

"Hello, mama," he said. "I brought her home as promised."

The Bene kissed his cheek. "Yes, you did, Kulal. I never doubted you."

Omolewa peeked up as the Bene stood. She was a tall woman, standing a few inches over Kulal.

"Everyone please rise," she said, her voice light yet firm. "Welcome to Zimbabwa. Welcome to Maputo. Welcome home."

She cradled Pik-Pik in her left arm while extending her right hand toward Omolewa.

"Daughter, will you come greet your mother?" she asked.

Omolewa looked at mama and baba.

"Go on Lewa," mama said. "Go on."

Omolewa climbed the stairs to stand before the Bene. Pik-Pik scampered back to her, sitting beside her feet. Omolewa took the Bene's hand and felt a tingle of familiarity. A warm sensation came to her forehead; she knew without looking her mark glowed for she saw the same pattern resonating on the Bene's forehead. Tears came to the Bene's eyes and Omolewa felt them on her own cheeks as well.

"My darling Lewa," the Bene whispered. "My beautiful, wonderful Lewa."

"Mama," Omolewa said. The word sprang from her mouth before she could stop it. She felt the bond, yet it was not the same as she felt for mama or for baba.

Suddenly the Bene fell to her knees then wrapped Omolewa into a fierce embrace.

"You look just as I dreamed you would," the Bene said. "I wish your father had lived to see you. He would have been so happy. So happy."

Omolewa returned the embrace.

"Mama and Baba have taken good care of me," she said.

The Bene's embrace relaxed. She pulled away from Omolewa, looking at her solemnly.

"Yes, they have," she said. "I wish we never sent you away, but it was necessary. But now you are home. I wish the circumstances were better, but we will make the best of it, won't we?"

"Yes," Omolewa agreed.

"Good. It makes me happy to hear you say that."

The Bene stood, her arm draped around Omolewa's shoulders.

"Tayari, come forward," she said. "Introduce me to the rest of your family."

Mama and Baba came up the stairs holding the little ones in their arms.

"It is good to see you again, Bene," Baba said. "You are as beautiful as you were the last day I saw you."

"Still the flatterer I see," the Bene replied. "And bold as ever."

She looked at Jamela with a knowing smile.

"Your husband was such the flirt," she said. "Rank did not matter to him. I thought my husband was going to have him executed."

Mama cut her eyes at baba. "Yes, he has his ways. But once he met me, he became a different man."

"A better man I would say."

The Bene and mama laughed.

"And who are the little ones?"

"Diwani and Kazija," mama said.

"You're tall!" Kazija blurted.

The Bene smiled. "Yes, I am, to a little one like you."

"To everybody!" Diwani replied.

They all laughed, Diwani's innocence breaking the tension.

"You are all my family as of this day," the Bene said. "I proclaim it so."

"It has been noted," Hajanika replied.

"Tayari will be honored as my brother, Jamela as my sister. Their children will be treated as my niece and nephew."

She looked at Omolewa, her eyes glistening again.

"And Omolewa takes her rightful place as my daughter."

"So it had been proclaimed, so it will be," Hajanika said.

The Bene looked at Omolewa and her family.

"Come with me."

She kept her arm around Omolewa's shoulders. Together they descended the dais then walked through the receiving room into the corridor. Omolewa had to walk briskly to keep up with the Bene and her lengthy strides.

"Where are we going?" Omolewa asked.

"To present you to the city," the Bene said.

They passed through the corridor and the atrium, the Bene's personal guard flanking them. As they emerged into the courtyard other guards fell in step with them. Their walk took them to a large platform attached to an arrangement of ropes and pulleys. The ropes were connected to a large winch harnessed to three large quaggats.

"What is that?" Omolewa asked the Bene.

"It is a lift," she replied. "It will take up to the ramparts."

Omolewa clutched the Bene's hands tighter.

"Is it safe?" she asked.

"I hope so. Otherwise this will be my last day as Bene."

It took Omolewa a moment to realize the Bene was teasing her. She smiled and the Bene laughed.

"Come, daughter. Let's take a ride."

Omolewa let the Bene lead her onto the platform. The others followed, baba, mama, and the little ones just as nervous as she. The guards seemed to sense their unease and formed a barrier between the royal entourage and the walled edge of the platform. A servant closed the platform door then prodded the quaggats with a long rod. The beasts walked and the platform jerked as the lift cable tightened ant the platform began its ascent. Omolewa pulled closer to the Bene as mama and baba picked up Diwani and Kazija and held them tight. The platform jerked to a halt; the guards opened the platform door then extended a ramp which connected the platform to the ramparts. The guards stepped out onto the wall first, followed by Omolewa and the Bene. They trailed the guards to a seating area situated over the gate. The Bene and Omolewa went to the front of the seating area as the guards lined up before them, each carrying a long staff topped with a square flag, the image of a leopard stitched onto a green background. A murmur of anticipation rose from below them; Omolewa leaned toward the guards but the Bene pulled her back.

"Not yet child," she said. "You'll ruin the spectacle."

The others filed in behind them and took their seats under the direction of Hajanika. Omolewa's family, Kulal and Kashta sat behind her and the Bene. The guards stood beside them, looking at the Bene. She nodded and the guards stepped forward in unison. The crowd cheered and the rampart drummers answered with a vigorous cadence. The Bene looked down at Omolewa and grinned.

"Are you ready?"

Omolewa swallowed hard. "I think so."

"Then let us step into your new future," the Bene said.

Omolewa and the Bene approached the edge of the wall. As they became visible the crowd cheered louder. The rampart drums were answered by the drummers in the crowd and a joyous conversation took place between them. The Bene's regal countenance took over, her jaw set stern, her eyes sweeping the crowd as if she saw each one of her subjects. She gripped Omolewa's hand then lifted it high with hers. When she spoke her resounding voice carried over the celebration din.

"Children of the Leopard! People of Zimbabwa! Mothers, fathers, brothers, sisters, aunts, uncles, cousins of Mutapa! Our family is whole! My daughter is home!"

Omolewa watched stunned as the crowd broke into dance and song. Although she did not understand the words, she could feel the emotion of them. All this for her? What was it that she possessed that made them all carry on so? Kashta told her of her potential but she still couldn't comprehend what would cause this amazing woman standing beside her and the hundreds of people below her carry on in such a way. As always Pik-Pik sensed her mood. She curled tighter around Omolewa's neck and licked her ear, her rough tongue tickling Omolewa and comforting her.

"I hope I live up to what they expect of me," she whispered.

The Bene looked down at Omolewa, apparently hearing her doubtful words.

"You will, my daughter," she replied. "I will make sure of it."

- 5 -

Omolewa sat at the table in her parent's room, picking at the bowl of stew before her. The room was bigger that their home in Nacala, containing a massive bed and a closet that was large enough for Diwani and Kazija to sleep in. Mama had requested a table set up for them to eat together and the Bene obliged. The servants struggled to bring the heavy wood table into the room but had not complained.

Mama and Baba whispered to each other as they ate, and Diwani and Kazija teased each other as always. Omolewa swirled her spoon in her stew then picked out morsels to share with Pik-Pik. The ferret lurked under her chair, waiting eagerly for the bits of meat and vegetables. Mama's voice broke her mood.

"Lewa? What is the matter?"

Omolewa looked up into mama's questioning eyes.

"This is all so much," she replied. "Too much."

"We understand," Baba said. "Come sit between us."

Omolewa carried her bowl to the opposite side of the table as Mama and Baba made room. Diwani and Kazija dragged her chair over, playing a game of tug of war with it along the way. Sitting between her parents helped her relax. She ate a few spoonfuls of stew before speaking.

"I don't know what they want from me," she said.

"Neither do we," mama replied.

"Whatever it is, I'm sure you can handle it," baba said. "You're my daughter."

"She's our daughter," mama corrected.

"No, I'm not," Omolewa said. The words came out on their own. The thought had been swirling in her head since she met the Bene. She then realized what had been bothering her.

"I'm not your child," she said. "I'm hers."

Mama hugged her.

"The Bene was the woman who gave birth to you," she said. "But we have raised you from a baby. We are just as much your parents as she is. And we love you just as much if not more."

"I know," Omolewa replied. "You have never hidden my origin from me. I look so different from you and baba and Diwani and Kazija. But I have never felt different…until now."

She looked at baba and mama, both with solemn expressions. She knew her words probably hurt them and she didn't want them to, but she had to say what she felt.

"Kulal looks like me. The Bene looks like me. When the Bene touches me, it feels familiar yet strange."

"Maybe things are moving a bit fast," baba said. "We will talk to the Bene. You need more time to get used to all this."

"I don't think I'll ever get used to all this," she replied.

"Always remember one thing Lewa," mama said. "We all love you. The Bene expressed her love for you by sending you away when your life was in danger. Baba and I demonstrated our love for you by taking you into our home and raising you as our own, which you are. You do not have to deal with this alone. We will help you."

The room echoed with a hard knock on the door. The door servant opened it and Kashta entered, a warm smile on his face.

"What a beautiful sight," he said. "You all are where you deserve to be."

Baba stood then greeted the mage.

"Join us please," he asked.

Kashta shook his head. "Thank you for offering but I must decline. I partook a small meal earlier and my constitution could not take any more."

"Zimbabwa food does not agree with you?" Baba asked.

"On the contrary, it agrees with me too much," Kashta replied. "I've gained too much weight since I've been here. Anymore and my family won't be able to recognize me when I return to Kamit."

"Sit with us at least," Baba said.

"Thank you again, but no. I'm only here to let Omolewa know that her training begins tomorrow."

"We would like Lewa to have a few more days before her training begins," baba said. "She is still trying to grasp all this."

Kashta frowned. "I know this is a lot to take in, but the sooner we begin the better. Omolewa has been away for a long time and she has much to learn."

"I'm not ready yet," Omolewa said.

"That is not for you to determine," Kashta replied.

"Wait a minute," baba said. "I understand the gravity of this situation…"

"No, you do not," Kashta said. "You don't understand it at all. None of you do."

An uncomfortable silence fell over the room. Diwani and Kazija were also quiet, looking at the grownups with nervous eyes.

"I'm going to have to ask you to leave," baba said. There was a tone in his voice Omolewa had never heard before. Kashta smirked as he looked baba up and down.

"You were a fine Mikijen in your day," Kashta said. "I've heard the stories about your skills. But don't fool yourself. It's been a long time since you've handled a blade, and even if you had one you've never confronted a man like me."

"We will ask the Bene," mama said as she stepped between the men. "She will decide what Lewa will do and when she will do it. Not us, and especially not you."

Kashta's frown deepened.

"So be it."

He spun about then stalked from the room, the guards closing the door behind him.

"That was not smart," mama said to baba. "He's a sonchai, a very powerful one at that."

"I don't care what he is," baba replied. "He won't tell us what to do. Lewa is our daughter. We will decide what she does and when she does it."

Omolewa could feel baba's anger. She touched his hand then smiled when he looked at her.

"It's okay baba," she said.

Baba smiled at her then picked her up like she was a little child. She hugged him tight.

"Who knew you would grow up to be so much trouble," he said.

"She's no trouble," mama said.

"Yes, she is," Diwani argued.

They all laughed as joy was restored to the room. They finished dinner then sat together before the fireplace as baba shared stories that he now remembered of Zimbabwa. Mama braided Omolewa's hair as they listened; Diwani and Kazija harassed Pik-Pik until the ferret took refuge in Omolewa's arms. They talked well into the night until the little ones fell asleep on the floor. Mama and Omolewa tucked them in.

Omolewa was walking to the door to go to her room when a wave of loneliness overcame her. She turned to her parents.

"Can I sleep here tonight?" she asked.

"Of course you can," mama said. "You can sleep with us. Eda knows this bed is big enough."

"It's big enough for all of us," baba said.

As if on cue Diwani and Kazija jumped from their beds, skittered across the floor then climbed into mama and baba's bed.

"We can all sleep together!" Kazija shouted.

Omolewa laughed as she climbed in the bed with mama and baba. As she snuggled in with her family, she felt more relaxed than she had in days. No matter what the Bene said, this was her family. They would always come first.

* * *

Morning was announced by a gentle tapping on the bedroom door. Omolewa pushed free of the tangle of bodies then sat up and rubbed her eyes. Pik-Pik peeked over the edge of the bed then scramble to her, climbing onto her shoulders and chattering in her ear.

"I'm hungry too," she answered.

Whoever was at the door tapped again. Omolewa looked at baba and mama for any motion then realized they were not about to wake up any time soon unless forced to. She decided to answer the door herself. She crawled from the bed then put on the thick robe given to them by the servants. The cotton was smooth and warm against her skin, almost enticing her to get back into bed for a few more minutes of sleep. Instead she made her way to the door then opened it. What she saw when she opened the door surprised her. She had expected one of the Bene's guards or at least one of her adult servants; instead she looked into the shocked brown eyes of a girl that seemed no older than she based on the smoothness of her sienna skin. Her hair was twisted in complex braids bundled into a ponytail resting on her shoulders. She wore a long blue kanga that scraped the top of her sandals. The shock gave way to a friendly smile as she bowed before Omolewa.

"Good morning, *mamoyo*," the girl said. "I am Palesa. The Bene sent me to let you know that you are to join her for breakfast. Please make sure you arrive soon."

"Thank you, Palesa," Omolewa replied. "What was that you called me?"

"*Mamoyo*," Palesa said. "It is the title of the Bene's daughter."

The girl bowed and hurried away. Omolewa went back to the bed then shook mama.

"Mama, mama, it's time to wake up."

Mama sat up then rubbed her eyes.

"Good morning," mama said. "Has breakfast arrived?"

"A girl named Palesa came," she said. "The Bene has invited us to have breakfast with her."

MILTON J DAVIS

"Oh my!" mama exclaimed. She reached over then shook baba hard.

"Wake up! The Bene wants to have breakfast with us!"

She looked at Omolewa.

"Wake up Diwani and Kazija and get them ready."

Omolewa groaned. Dealing with those two in the morning was a special kind of torture. Omolewa pushed her brother and sister awake then suffered through the whining and fake crying as she dressed them and washed their faces. Then she had to endure their playing and teasing as mama and baba dressed. Luckily, they were in a hurry, so the ritual didn't last as long as usual. When they stepped out the room a group of servants waited, including Palesa. The girl came to stand beside her.

"What is this?" Omolewa asked.

"Nothing, *mamoyo*," Palesa replied.

"So why are you walking with me?" she asked.

Palesa lowered her head. "I can walk behind you if you wish."

"No, no!" Omolewa said, suddenly embarrassed. "I didn't mean it that way. I thought you were walking with me because you had something to say."

Palesa grinned. "The Bene has assigned me to you. I am to help you adjust to life in the palace."

"You are my servant?"

Palesa nodded. "Yes, mamayo."

"Thank you," Omolewa said. "And you don't need to call me mamoyo. My family calls me Lewa."

"I will have to ask the Bene," Palesa said. "She is very firm on protocol."

"Then let's have our own agreement," Omolewa said. "When in formal settings you can call me mamoyo. When it is the two of us Lewa will do."

Palesa smiled. "I like that. I like it very much. You are not like the others."

"No," Omolewa said. "I'm not."

The servants led them down the corridor to a room near the Bene's greeting hall. A large table filled most of it, its

68

surface covered with food. The Bene sat at the head of the table flanked by Kulal and Hajanika. Kashta sat beside Kulal, a forced smile on his face. The Kamite sonchai's demeanor had changed since they came to Zimbabwa. His fatherly manner and kind words had been replaced by an impatient nature. Omolewa looked away from him to the Bene as she bowed before sitting. The Bene waved her hand, dismissing Omolewa's gesture.

"None of that here," she said. "You are among family. Did you rest well?"

"Yes, we did," mama said.

"Despite the fact you shared the same bed?" the Bene asked.

"It's not the first time," baba replied.

The Bene tilted her head. "Interesting."

She did not seem to be in approval of it, but her smile quickly returned.

"I've been told there has been some disagreement of when Omolewa should begin her studies."

"Yes, it has," baba said. "Only months ago, Lewa learned of her status and now we are here. She needs time to adjust."

"I can see that being an issue," the Bene replied. "But you must understand our situation. There are forces gathering that mean to do great harm not only to Zimbabwa but to Ki Khanga. This is not a just a feeling or a possibility; this is a fact. When that day comes, we all must be ready to do our part. As people of lineage, we have been granted great privilege and power by Eda, but with that privilege comes greater responsibility. We serve the people just as much as they serve us. Now is time for us to serve."

The Bene's eyes were on Omolewa the entire time she spoke. It was if her words struck her heart like blows and shook loose a feeling of shame. This couldn't just be a normal response. Omolewa suspected the Bene worked some charm on her to make her feel this way.

"I have not had such privileges in my life," she said. "I just need some time."

"We will discuss this later," the Bene said. "Let's eat before the food gets cold."

The mood lightened as they ate, Diwani and Kazija working their magic with silly talk and comical expressions. All eyes kept finding their way to Omolewa, and she tried her best to stay pleasant during the meal. When the servants arrived to clear the table Omolewa stood quickly, ready to leave. The Bene stood with her.

"Omolewa, will you walk with me?" she asked.

Fear tightened Omolewa's throat. Her answer was strained.

"Yes, Bene."

The Bene glanced at mama and baba and they nodded their approval. Omolewa walked to the head of the table, Palesa behind her. Hajanika was rising to her feet when the Bene shook her head.

"Stay," the Bene said. "You too, Palesa."

Omolewa and the Bene left the dining hall and entered the corridor.

"Tell me your thoughts," the Bene said.

Omolewa cleared her throat. "This is all so much. Kashta explained to me some of what is happening and I want to help. Well, I think I do. I wish I had a choice. I mean I want a choice."

The Bene nodded. "When I was your age, I felt the same. As a child being the Bene's daughter was a wonderful thing. I was denied nothing. I wore the best clothes and received the most wonderful gifts for my birthday. My siblings and I loved each other very much. I could not imagine how life could be any better. I did not know then I was living the best years of my life."

They entered the atrium. The cool damp air reminded Omolewa of Nacala, so much so she almost expected to look out and see dhow sails in the distance. Instead she was greeted by the towering flowered shrubs.

"Sooner or later childhood ends and we must step into the responsibilities of adulthood," the Bene continued. "In Zimbabwa boys and girls take part in a ritual that marks the day of that transition. They are given tasks that require them to prove they are ready. If they fail, they are not able to marry or leave the family compound. For me and my siblings, failure meant not being considered to rule Zimbabwa when the time came."

"We have no such thing among the Kiswala," Omolewa said. "Mama was teaching me how to cook and baba taught me his carpentry trade. I was also given responsibility of Diwani and Kazija. I would rather build a dhow than take care of them."

The Bene laughed. "See, the Kiswala have their own rituals."

The Bene sat on a stone bench that rested under the branches of a tree filled with ripe red fruit Omolewa didn't recognize. She sat beside the Bene.

"This is a burden you did not expect, but it is a responsibility that you were destined for. Your father came to us in a time of war. The Elders had chosen me as Bene after my mother died. My brothers were not happy about the decision. They challenged my selection and when the Elders upheld their decision they left Maputo with bitterness. Two years later we were at war."

"Why did they get so angry with you?" Omolewa asked. "I thought you loved each other."

The Bene's shoulders slumped as her eyes glistened. "People change, even those closest to you. My brothers had always teased me about being my parents' favorite but I thought nothing of it. I didn't realize they believed it to be true and resented it. They also did not like the fact that it was I who inherited the strongest lineage ashé."

"You mean the talents I possess?"

"Yes. I did not understand how they could hate me about a thing that I had no control over. But like I said, people change."

The Bene reached up and picked a fruit from the tree then handed it to Omolewa.

"Thank you, Bene, but I am not hungry."

"This is not about hunger," the Bene said. "Taste it."

Omolewa bit the fruit. No sooner did her teeth touch its skin did she feel a surge of energy that caused her to fall off the bench. She remained on the ground, staring at the fruit.

"What…what was that?" she said.

"People are not the only things that possess ashé," the Bene said. "It exists in animals, plants and minerals. The shumba you encountered on your way to Maputo is a prime example. They are known for their ashé which is why they are hunted by lesser sonchai. This atrium is filled with plants and other creatures that possess powerful ashé. Their presence alone will replenish you. To consume a part of any of them will revive you. This tree, the Upenyu, is the most powerful of all. Its fruit is filled with ashé, yet no seed from it will sprout into a new tree until the parent tree dies. This palace was built around this tree. It is centuries old."

Omolewa looked at the fruit in her hand then into the Bene's eyes.

"My training has begun."

The Bene smiled. "Yes, it has."

She returned to sit by her birth mother.

"I need you to pay attention to Kashta. He valuable knowledge about the threat we face. The Kamites are an industrious people but their ashé is modest compared to ours. They make up for it with their inventions. Kashta is an exception."

"So you trust him?" Omolewa asked.

"Yes, as much as I can trust anyone. We are allies in this threat. We must work together as much as possible. Kulal has trained among them. He spent three years in Kamit and learned much. I was hoping you could go as well but time is short."

Omolewa bit into the upenya fruit again. This time she felt a slight rush.

"The first bite is always the most intense," the Bene said.

"I have many questions for you," Omolewa said.

"And I have many answers, but not today. Today I would like you to go with Kashta to his academy and begin your studies. Will you do this?"

"I will," Omolewa said. It wasn't as if she had a choice. It was obvious that there was no turning back. They would not let her or her family go back to Nacala until she trained to use this ashé she possessed.

"I want to know more of this threat," she continued. "Twice my life has been threatened. I want to know why and who is doing this."

"We will tell you when it is time," the Bene said.

"And I want to know your name."

The Bene laughed. "I will share it with you, but you must never use it before others."

Omolewa nodded. "I won't."

"My name is Anadina."

"It is a pretty name."

"I think so," the Bene said. She picked another fruit from the tree and began eating.

"When we return, you will go with Kashta, okay?"

"Yes, Bene."

"Good. Now let's finish our snack then get about our day."

They ate the fruit in silence, Omolewa marveling at the energy it supplied to her. There was lightness to her step as they walked back to the dining hall.

"I have some clothes for you if you would like to see them," the Bene said.

"So soon?" Omolewa replied.

"They were my clothes when I was your age," the Bene said. "Titles aren't the only thing we pass down. These garments are made by special weavers that only serve our lineage. The fabrics they weave are designed to enhance your skills as well. The threads are treated with special medicines known only to weavers and shared only with us."

"Does Kulal wear these garments?" she asked.

"Yes, he does," the Bene said. The smile left her face at the mention of Kulal.

"There is one more thing I must tell you," she said. "It's best you know now so you won't experience the pain I did."

"What is it?"

"Kulal is a loving son," she said. "No one is closer to my heart than him. I hope you will be as close one day."

Omolewa said nothing. She would not promise that which she did not know she could give, at least not yet.

"Remember the story I told you of my brothers? It is for that reason you must be observant of Kulal. He is very fond of you, but those feelings could change as you grow into who you were meant to be."

"I don't want anything he has," Omolewa said. "He has no reason to fear me."

"Heed my words," the Bene said. "They are hard for me to say but they need to be said."

When they returned the dining hall was empty of everyone except Kashta. Gone was the judgmental expression he'd possessed over the past few days. In its place was the fatherly countenance Omolewa has experienced on the journey to Zimbabwa.

"I see you have discussed Omolewa's responsibilities," he said.

"Yes, we have," the Bene said. "She will accompany you to the academy today."

"That is excellent news!"

The Bene bent over then kissed Omolewa's cheek. It felt odd for this woman to kiss her in such a way but she did not protest.

"Be diligent," the Bene said. "You have much to learn and little time to do so."

"Yes, Bene," Omolewa replied.

"Come now," Kashta said. "We waste the day."

Omolewa followed Kashta down the corridor, through the atrium then into the courtyard.

"I take it the Bene introduced you to the upenya tree?" he asked.

"Yes. It was very…unique."

"Good. You will need its energy today. Our lesson will be quite strenuous."

They entered a door on the rampart walls. Inside the room were objects of various shapes and sizes, some as small as a marble and others the size of boulders.

"Today we will begin your focus and control exercises," Kashta said. "You possess tremendous ashé but you must learn to control and manipulate it. Remember what Kulal did with the shumba?"

Omolewa shivered at the mention of the beast. "Yes, I do."

"You will be able to that and so much more," Kashta replied. "But first you must find your ashé before you can control it."

"Find it? I have used it before."

Kashta grinned. "And how do you use it? How do you summon it?"

"I don't know," she answered. "I just do."

"And that is what we must change," he said. "All creatures have certain abilities that are born within them. Walking, eating, breathing; these are abilities granted to us by Eda. But there are some skills we must learn. You can be born with grace, but still you must be taught to dance. You may be born with quick reflexes, but still you must learn to fight. Natural ability will only get you so far. In order to excel, you must be taught."

They sat before a small table. Before them sat a tray filled with balls arranged according to their size. The smallest was the size of her thumbnail, the largest the size of her fist.

"Now lift the smallest ball," Kashta said.

Omolewa reached for the ball.

"No. Not with your hand. With your ashé."

Omolewa pulled her hand closer to her. Her eyebrows bunched as she concentrated on the small ball. Moments later it shot into the air, smashing into the ceiling then falling back to the table.

"I'm sorry," Omolewa said. "That has never happened before!"

"It's the upenya," Kashta said. "I must say I have never seen it boost someone's abilities so much so soon."

Omolewa didn't know if Kashta's words were a compliment or a concern.

"Let us try one more time," he said. "This time I want you go more slowly. Before you lift the ball, I want you to touch it only."

Omolewa took a breath then reached out with her ashé. The ball trembled as she 'felt' it. Its surface was textured like that of the dock workers, palms and fingers calloused from the ropes and crates they pulled and lifted every day.

"I feel it," she said.

"Good," Kashta replied. "Imagine holding the ball as if you were holding it with your fingers. Turn it slowly."

Omolewa attempted to turn the ball. It shook violently then shattered into splinters. She yelped as a small shard glanced her cheek.

"My goodness!" Kashta exclaimed. "This is most amazing!"

Omolewa touched her cheek where the shard grazed her. She was bleeding. Kashta noticed the wound as well.

"I will send for a healer," he said. He was walking away from the table then turned to smile at her.

"When you have mastered your skills, you won't need one."

He called for a servant then returned to the room.

"We will have to devise new exercises for you," he said. "I would also advise you to stay away from the upenya for now. We must make sure your manipulation skills are advanced before you can enhance your ashé. Come with me, we will go to the classroom and return after the enhancement has subsided."

Omolewa followed Kashta from the training room and back into the courtyard. This time they walked toward the gate. The guards saw them approaching and immediately opened it.

"Where are we going?" Omolewa asked.

"We're going to school," he said.

"I thought I was to be trained within the palace," she said.

"For some things, yes. Have you been to school before?"

"No. Mama and baba could not afford it. They taught me at home. I can read and write Kiswala. I know a few words of Tradespeak, and I can add and subtract."

"I suspected as much," Kashta answered. "This school with get you up to speed with the fundamentals. Once you have tested out, I will oversee your higher learning. The Zimbabwa are learned people, but no country in Ki Khanga matches Kamit when it comes to higher education."

Omolewa grinned. "Are you sure?"

Kashta looked at her with a frown. "I'm positive."

Omolewa covered her mouth as she laughed. Kashta eyebrows rose then he smiled.

"Ah, you tease your elder."

"I'm sorry. I couldn't help it."

"Don't apologize. It's rather refreshing. It reminds me of my students in Kamit."

"Do you miss your home?" she asked.

"Yes, I do," Kashta said. "I thought I would miss the technology most, but I don't. What I miss most is my family and friends."

"Are you married?" she asked.

"No," he replied. "I would have never taken on this duty if I had a family."

"I understand," she said. "I have a family, too."

Kashta grinned again. "You are wise beyond your years. We both do what we have to do, not necessarily what we want to do."

They reached the academy. The building was built of marble from the nearby quarry, a pristine ivory colored structure decorated with spiraling patterns around the carved doors and windows. Voices of children reciting mathematical equations seeped through the closed door. Kashta knocked and the door opened, revealing a tall woman draped in a red robe and matching headwrap. The woman nodded at Kashta then shared a wide smile with Omolewa.

"Welcome, mamoyo," she said. "I'm *Mudzidzisi* Mudiwa Gonzo. We were so excited when we learned you would be attending our academy. Please, come inside."

They entered the classroom. The children stood then prostrated before Omolewa, catching her off guard.

"Please, you don't have to do that," she said.

"They are showing their respect for you and the Bene," Mudiwa said. "Please allow them to do so."

The children stood then returned to their seats. They ranged in age, from as young as Kazija to some older than Omolewa.

"This is your seat," Mudiwa said. She led Omolewa to a seat in the first row. Omolewa was not happy; this meant she would have to pay attention whether she wished to or not. She looked at Kashta and he gave her a sly grin.

"The mamoyo is honored to be among your students," Kashta said. "Your teaching skills are well known and respected. We trust that you will do a fantastic job bringing the mamoyo to the appropriate level for her age range."

"I will do my best," Mudiwa replied. "We are reciting mathematical facts."

Mudiwa went to her desk then returned with a tablet.

"Are you familiar with theses, mamoyo?"

Omolewa studied the tablet. "Yes I am. My mama taught me at home."

"Good. We are reciting from the beginning to the end. We will start over so you can recite with us."

"I leave her in your hands," Kashta said. "I will send Palesa for you when it is time for you to return, Omolewa."

Omolewa took her seat in front of the class.

"Okay, let's resume from the beginning."

Omolewa recited the equations, her voice more confident with each fact. After the recital they worked on new problems. Omolewa was familiar with these as well, so the first day in class was easy. Once the lessons were finished the other children crowded around her, asking so many questions that Omolewa was exhausted by the time Palesa arrived. She was relieved to see her. They walked side by side to the palace, their guards walking behind them.

"So did you enjoy your day at school?" Palesa asked.

"Yes," Omolewa said. "I realized what a good job mama has done teaching me. I was able to keep up with the others. Do you go to school, Palesa?"

"No. My parents were not able to afford it before I became a servant. Now I have no time."

Omolewa didn't like the fact that Palesa's duties prevented her from studying.

"Tomorrow I will ask the Bene if you can come with me," she said.

Palesa's eyes went wide. "Mamoyo, that is not necessary!"

"Yes, it is," Omolewa said. "You can come and learn with me. What you don't know I can teach you."

"Are you sure?" Palesa asked.

"Of course, I am. We will learn together."

Palesa smiled. "As you wish, mamoyo."

"I wish it," Omolewa said. "And stop calling me that. It's Lewa, remember."

"Yes, I remember. Thank you, Lewa."

Kashta waited for them at the entrance of the gate.

"I take it your class went well?" he asked.

"Yes. There was nothing done that I wasn't familiar with."

"Good. You parents taught you well."

Omolewa smiled. "Speaking of my parents, I would like to see them now."

"Of course. Palesa will take you to them. Afterwards we will meet in the dining hall."

Omolewa shared a weak smile. She was looking forward to a meal alone with her family. These formal dinners were not comfortable to her. She followed Palesa to her parents' room.

"You do not wish to take dinner with the others," Palesa said.

"No, I don't."

"I do not see why," she replied. "Being the presence of the Bene is a privilege."

"Maybe for you but not for me," Omolewa said. "All this is taking time to settle in."

"It was a joyous day when you returned to us. Many would be disappointed if they knew you did not feel the same."

"I didn't know I was the Bene's daughter until a few months ago. How can I be happy about something I never knew existed? And how could you be joyous? You are no older than I."

They stopped before her parents' room.

"We are a proud people," Palesa said. "The Bene is our family. When one of us is happy, we are all happy. I think in time you will feel as we do."

Palesa knocked on the door.

"The mamoyo has returned," she announced.

The door jerked open; Diwani and Kazija rushed out and grabbed Omolewa's hands.

"Lewa! Come play with us!"

They dragged Lewa into the room. Mama and baba sat at a small table resting at the end of their bed, smiling as she approached them. Baba looked over her shoulder at Palesa.

"That will be all for now Palesa," he said.

Palesa nodded.

"I will wait for you at your chamber," she said.

Omolewa nodded and Palesa left the room. She hugged her parents then sat at the table with them.

"Kashta tells us you show great promise," mama said.

"He said you ashé is the most powerful he's seen as such a young age," baba said.

"Uh huh," Omolewa replied.

"Is something wrong?" mama asked.

"I'm still not comfortable with all this mama," she replied. "I use what I have to help us. Now I'm expected to use it to help all these people, people I don't even know."

"Then maybe you should get to know them," baba said.

"Get to know them? How will I do that?"

"Ever since we've arrived you've been surrounded by family and servants," he said. "Maybe we should get out and walked the streets of Maputo and visit the market."

"Do you think the Bene would let us do that?" Omolewa asked. She missed going to market with mama. Although she had no idea what the Maputo market possessed, she was sure it would be exciting.

"She would probably have us surrounded by guards and servants," mama said.

"I could be your guard," baba said. "And Palesa could come with us."

"Do you think the Bene would let us have our own house too?" Omolewa asked.

"It would be nice to have a home of our own," baba said.

"We will ask her at dinner tonight," mama said.

"Yes, we will," baba said.

A servant came to the room later to announce dinner. Omolewa and her family strolled to the dining hall and were greeted by the Bene, Kulal and Kashta. They talked of Omolewa's first day of training, then Kulal and the Bene discussed palace business. Baba waited until the business of the day had been discussed before he spoke.

"Bene, is it possible for us to have a house of our own?"

The Bene's eyes widened.

"What is the matter?" she asked. "Is there something that has occurred in the palace that I should be aware of?"

"No Bene," mama said. "We are grateful for your hospitality and everything you have done for us. It's just that we would like to have a home of our own."

"This is your home," the Bene said.

"It is a nice thought," baba said. "But in reality, it's not. It's yours."

"They want their privacy," Kulal said.

"Yes," baba said.

The Bene looked at Omolewa.

"And I take it if you had this home Omolewa would live with you."

Baba's expression turned serious.

"Yes, she would."

"I must think about this," she said. "I understand your need for privacy, yet these are not normal circumstances. Omolewa is special. She needs close supervision and guidance."

"Haven't we provided that since she was born?" mama said.

"Yes, you have," the Bene answered. "But circumstances are different now. Her life has been threatened."

"We are in Maputo, the capital of Zimbabwa," Baba said. "I don't think she could get any safer."

"He has a point," Kulal said.

The Bene looked at Kashta.

"What do you think?"

"I think we must be cautious," he said. "Those who wish to thwart our plans have eyes and ears everywhere and Omolewa is not completely sensitive to them. I would recommend that she stay in the palace until her training has progressed sufficiently."

"And how long will that take?" baba asked.

"I don't know," Kashta replied. "From what I saw today, not long at all."

"I could have told you that," Kulal said.

"I will grant you a home, something close to the palace," the Bene decided. "Omolewa will reside at the palace to make sure her training is progressing well. Once Kashta is satisfied she can stay at the home with you. When her training is complete, she can decide where she wishes to reside permanently."

Baba and mama did not seem happy with the Bene's decision. Omolewa knew she wasn't. Still, they nodded in agreement.

"It is settled then," Kashta said.

Omolewa spent the night again in her parents' room. As she snuggled close to them, worry crowded her thoughts. She felt as if she was losing control, as if her life was being taken from her. Though mama and baba told her what to do, she never felt as she felt now. There was something about it all that was not right. She didn't know exactly what it was, but it worried her like a splinter that couldn't be removed.

She sighed as she laid her head against mama's back. Now was the time to rest. Tomorrow would surely be a busy day.

- 6 -

The new day began as the first with Omolewa and her family
sharing breakfast with the Bene, Kulal, Kashta and Hajanika.
But this day would be different. Mama and Baba set out with
her siblings to find a new home for them outside the palace
walls. Omolewa was excited for them; at last, they would
have a place of their own, even if she would not be able to
spend every day with them. She met Kashta at the training
room and resumed her manipulation exercises. As Kashta
suspected the objects were easier to control without the influence of the upenya fruit. She lifted each ball with ease except
the largest. Omolewa strained to elevate it, the effort igniting
a sharp pain behind her forehead.

"Why does this make my head ache?" she asked
Kashta.

"Because your ashé is intertwined with your body,"
he said. "Your ashé is a part of you, just like your fingers and
toes."

"But you said it comes from my lineage and my ancestors," she replied.

"It does, yet it is still connected to your body and your
mind. That is why it is important that you stay physically and
mentally fit. The stronger your body, the stronger your physical manipulations. The stronger your mind, the stronger your
reasoning power."

Omolewa sat then drank her water. "So a man's ashé
is stronger than a woman's?"

"No," Kashta said. "Remember, the strength of ashé
is based on physical, mental and spiritual balance. The better

the balance, the stronger the ashé. And then there is of course inheritance."

"How does that factor?" she asked.

"Eda blesses us all differently," he said. "You can see it in humans as well as the creatures of the bush. Some simbas are stronger than others; some faru are faster than others. They are not all the same, and neither are we. We have no say so in what we will or will not be granted, but we can influence our outcome no matter what Eda blesses us with."

A servant entered the room with a bowl of upenya fruit. Omolewa smiled at Kashta.

"I knew today would be taxing," he said. "The fruit is meant to replenish. The stronger you become, the less you'll need it."

Omolewa bit into the sweet fruit and immediately felt the fatigue dissipate and her headache subside.

"You said we can influence our outcome," she said. "How do we do this?"

"You already have," Kashta said. "How did you discover your skills?"

Omolewa thought back to the day she first realized she possessed her gift.

"I was very little," she said. "Baba was working and mama and I were at the market selling baskets. Well, she was selling baskets. I was playing by myself. I had a ball that I would bounce and catch. Sometimes I would miss it and it would roll from behind the stand. Mama got mad at me and told me the next time it rolled away it would stay there. Well, I bounced it, missed catching it and it rolled away. I didn't want to lose my ball, but I knew mama would not let me go after it. So I shouted, 'come back!' And it did."

Omolewa ate another upenya. She felt refreshed and ready to continue her training.

"I had a new game," she continued. "I'd roll the ball toward the street then yell, 'come back!' Mama finally looked back at me with a frown then asked me what I was doing. I showed her. I'd never seen her so frightened in my life. She quickly shut down our stall then hurried us home. When Baba returned, she made me show him. He didn't seem as frightened as mama; it was as if he expected it to happen."

"You are correct," Kashta replied. "He did expect it."

"Kashta, why is it that my baba knew some things and not others?" she asked. "And where is the Bene's husband? Did he die?"

"Those are questions you must ask the Bene," Kashta said. "You deserve the answers and she deserves the right to give them to you. For now, we will continue your manipulation exercises. We have a few things to cover before you go to the academy."

The rest of the session was much less taxing. Palesa met Omolewa and together they walked to the academy. When they reached the entrance Palesa turned to leave.

"No Palesa," Omolewa said. "Remember what I said yesterday?"

Palesa eyes widened. "I didn't think you were serious."

"I was. Come inside with me."

They entered the building together. The children rose from their seats and prostrated immediately as the *mudzidzisi* approached.

"Hello Omolewa!" she said. "Who is your friend?"

"I am Palesa, mudzidzisi. I am Omolewa's servant."

"Good. You will sit beside Omolewa. Maybe you will learn a thing or two as well."

Palesa eye brightened and she smiled. "I hope so."

"Mudzidzisi, can you ask the class to stop doing that when I come to class?"

"They only mean to honor you."

Omolewa frowned. "I know, but they have honored me once already."

The children laughed and Omolewa stuck out her tongue at them, which made them laugh louder.

"As you wish," the mudzidzisi said. "Now take your seat. We have new equations to learn today."

As they walked to the seat Palesa leaned close to her.

"I don't know what to do," she whispered.

"It's okay," Omolewa whispered back. "Just say what I say for now. When we get back, I'll have mama explain it to you. She's very smart."

The two sat and the lessons began. Omolewa recited the new equations as Palesa stood beside her silent with a generous smile on her face. This day the mudzidzisi gave them problems to work on based on their new equations. Omolewa worked them out slowly, explaining each one to Palesa along the way.

"Try it," Omolewa said.

Palesa shook her head. "I'm not ready."

"They only way you'll be ready is to try," Omolewa said. "You probably won't get it right the first time but that is how you learn."

Palesa accepted the chalk from Omolewa then worked on the problem. She huffed then slammed the chalk on the board.

"I'm can't do it!" she said. "I'm stupid!"

"No, you're not," Omolewa said. "You were almost there. You gave up to soon. Mama says the toughest part of climbing a mountain is when you're closest to the peak. Let's do it together."

Omolewa talked Palesa through the problem. As they figured out the solution Palesa's bright smile returned.

"See, I told you you could do it," Omolewa said.

"I couldn't without your help," Palesa replied.

"You'll get it right the next time."

They worked problems for the rest of the class. Palesa picked up quickly; by the end of class she was working on her own. The mudzidzisi rang her bell and the younger students collect the boards. The mudzidzisi came to Omolewa.

"You are a very good helper," she said. "You will make a great Bene one day."

The mudzidzisi's words sobered Omolewa's mood. She'd never considered the fact that the Bene might be training her to take the stool one day. She'd always assumed that honor would go to Kulal. But then she also remembered what the Bene told her, that the person who became Bene was chosen by the Elders, and those elders did not always choose the oldest heir.

"Thank you, mudzidzisi," she said. "I think my . . . brother is far more qualified for that role."

"*Nevanji* Kulal is a great man," the mudzidzisi said. "We shall see when the time comes."

Omolewa felt a bit unnerved as they left the academy.

"Let's not go back just yet," she said to Palesa.

"They are expecting us," Palesa said. "If we don't return soon the Bene will send guards to look for us."

"I don't feel like returning right now," Omolewa said. "Do you know the way to the market?"

"Yes, but . . ."

"Let's go," Omolewa said. "The Bene said once I get to know the people of Mutapa I would feel more comfortable here."

"I don't think this is wise, Omolewa," Palesa warned.

"We will only stay a moment."

Palesa eyes shifted about.

"As you wish," she finally said.

She grabbed Omolewa's hand then led her away from the palace. Omolewa was happy for Palesa's guidance. If she had attempted to go on her own, she would have been completely lost. Mutapa was a much larger city than Nacala and there were many compounds for the various families and cultures that called the city home. But soon she heard the familiar din and caught the aroma of a nearby market.

"This is the Bene's market," Palesa said. "It is the largest in Mutapa. It's where we come for supplies, at least those that are not delivered directly to the palace. It is the best market in the city."

Palesa seemed to have relaxed more as they entered the market. Omolewa turned her face away from a trio of palace guards wading through the crowd; Palesa did the same.

"I will be in so much trouble when we return," Palesa said.

"No, you won't," Omolewa replied. "I will. You are my servant. I ordered you to take me."

"It won't make a difference," Palesa said.

"Let's not worry about that now," Omolewa said. "Let's enjoy the market."

Palesa led her to a stall where a portly man sold grilled goat and yams on a skewer. Omolewa purchased one for her and Palesa. The goat was extra spicy, forcing them to quickly find a vendor that sold mango juice and chimodho. They sipped on their nectar from narrow necked gourds and nibbled on their bread as they indulged in the abundance of the market. The two argued over which ream of cloth at one of the fabric vendors stalls was the most beautiful, then they tasted seasonings from the far reaches of Ki Khanga at the spice vendor. The jewelers shooed them away; she was only interested in the wealthier looking patrons and their garments didn't reflect their status. They came upon an elderly woman, a henna artist, who painted patterns on hands; Palesa and Omolewa had their hands decorated with matching symbols. They were strolling along a narrow street when Palesa tugged Omolewa's arm.

"Look!" she said.

"Where?" Omolewa replied.

"Over at the jeweler's stall. That boy is looking at you."

Omolewa casually peered toward the stall. A tall boy with bright eyes smiled at her as he nodded his head.

"I think he recognized me!" Omolewa said. She grabbed Palesa's hand. "Come, we must go!"

Palesa took the lead. The boy's smile faded, and he began walking toward them.

"Faster!" Omolewa said.

The two of them jostled through the crowd as the boy gained ground. His smile returned as he was almost to them, reaching out his hand to touch Omolewa. With no other recourse left to her, Omolewa screamed. The boy jerked his hand back, shocked by her reaction. He began to open his mouth when a market constable jumped between him and Omolewa.

"What is going on here?" the constable said. "This is the Bene's market! There will be no…mamoyo! What are you doing here unescorted!"

Before Omolewa could reply the constable pulled a small horn from his waist and blew three sharp notes. In moments she and Palesa were surrounded by palace guards.

"We will escort you back to the palace," the guard said. He gave Palesa a mean stare.

"It's not her fault," Omolewa replied. "I requested her to."

"Please, mamoyo, follow me," he said.

Omolewa, Palesa and their circlet of guards marched through the market, drawing the attention of all around. Some seemed annoyed by the disruption, others curious as to what was going on. Omolewa dared to look between the guards and saw the boy looking at them with a disappointed expression. An older man with elegant dress appeared at his side and began scolding him as he pulled him away. Her gaze was interrupted by Palesa's worried voice.

"The Bene will punish me!" she said.

"No, she won't," Omolewa replied. "I won't let her."

"You won't be able to stop her," Palesa replied. "She is the Bene! She will punish you, too."

"I don't think she will," Omolewa said. "I am still new to her. She will let me have my way a little while longer."

"How do you know this? You do not understand her," Palesa said.

Omolewa gave Palesa a sly grin. "I know adults."

Palesa's expression didn't change. "There is a side of the Bene you have not seen yet."

"What are you talking about?"

"A ruler must be fair and just," Palesa said. "She must also be harsh, and sometimes cruel."

Omolewa stomach tightened inside. "All we did was go to the market."

"We disobeyed the Bene," Palesa said. "People have died doing so. Even her own husband."

Omolewa jerked still, stunned by Palesa's words. "What?"

The guards walking behind them almost ran into them.

"Mamoyo, pardon us. Please continue to the palace."

Omolewa continued walking, albeit much slower.

"How do you know this?" she asked Palesa. "Who would do such a thing?"

"I will say no more," Palesa said.

Kashta and Kulal waited for them as they reached the palace gates. Neither looked happy. As they entered, the guards broke their protective ring then prostrated before Kulal. The guard Omolewa assumed to be the senior spoke.

"*Nevanji*, we responded to a market constable distress call and discovered the mamoyo in the market with her servant. They seemed to be in danger, so we came to their aid."

"Thank you, Kudzani," Kulal said. "You and your men may return to your stations. You will be rewarded. The mamoyo apologizes for this unexpected situation."

Kulal stared at Omolewa then gave her a slight nod.

"I am sorry," she said to the guard.

Kudzani smiled. "No apologies necessary, mamoyo. I am here to serve you."

The men came to their feet them marched away.

"What were you thinking?" Kashta said. "Of all the places you choose for distraction you pick the most dangerous!"

"Calm down," Kulal said. "This has been a hard transition. I can understand Lewa wanted to get away from all this."

Kulal winked at her, and she smiled. He really liked her. She couldn't imagine any situation where they would become enemies. She would make sure it never happened.

"Don't defend her," Kashta said. "What she did was…"

"What was it Kashta," Kulal asked. "Remember, this is the mamoyo of who you speak of."

Kashta folded his arms as frustration claimed his countenance.

"It was unwise," he finally said.

"Nevertheless, it happened," Kulal said. "But I suspect it won't happen again."

"No, it won't," Omolewa answered.

"Still, there will be a price to pay."

Kulal turned and began ambling across the courtyard.

"The Bene and your parents are waiting for you."

Omolewa mood dropped like a bucket down a well. She heard Palesa sigh. They trudged behind Kulal and Kashta into the palace, through the atrium, down the long corridor and eventually to the dining hall. The Bene, mama and baba sat at the table. None of them were smiling. Diwani, Kazija and Pik-Pik ran up to her. Pik-Pik climbed up to her neck then curled up against it. Diwani and Kazija pressed against her legs, Diwani looking up with sympathetic eyes.

"You're in trouble," he said.

"Palesa. Leave us," the Bene said.

"Yes Bene."

Palesa hurried from the dining hall. Omolewa watched her until she disappeared.

"What will you do to her?" she asked.

"Palesa is not your concern," the Bene said.

"What you did was extremely foolish," mama said. "So many things could have happened!"

"This is not Nacala," baba said. "And even if it was you would know better to let us know where you were."

"I'm sorry," she said. "I just needed some time to relax."

"Then you should have told someone," Mama said. "I'm very disappointed in you. Very disappointed."

"If you were younger, you know what would happen," baba said. The Bene cut her eyes at papa. If he was aware of it, he did not seem to be.

"You are a young woman, and we expect better of you," mama said. "You have responsibilities now that cannot be taken lightly."

"Yes, mama," Omolewa said. "I understand."

"Do you?" mama said. "I don't think so."

The disappointment in mama's voice hurt her more than any switch would. She looked to the Bene's eyes and saw that she agreed with everything her mother said.

"You will take your lessons within the palace from now on," the Bene said. "If you wish to travel beyond the palace, you will do so with an escort. You must never be alone outside these walls. Do you understand?"

"Yes Bene," Omolewa said. "I understand."

She hesitated for a moment before asking the question that burned inside her.

"What will happen to Palesa?"

"She will be punished," the Bene said.

"How?"

"That is not your concern. We will assign a new servant."

"I don't want a new servant," Omolewa said.

"That is not your decision to make," the Bene said. "Now let's take our meal before it gets cold."

Omolewa went to her chair then sat. Diwani sat beside her.

"I told you you were in trouble," he said.

"Be quiet and eat," Omolewa said.

The dinner was consumed in tense silence. Omolewa wasn't so concerned about her punishment; it was Palesa that worried her most. Afterwards when they returned to her parents' room she did not go inside.

"I think I'll stay in my room tonight," she announced.

"I know you're upset," baba began. "You don't have to be alone, though."

"Let her go," mama said.

"I want to stay with Lewa!" Kazija said.

"Me, too!" Diwani shouted.

"You two will stay with us," mama answered. "We'll see you in the morning, Lewa. Good night."

"Good night."

She entered her bedroom, her first time seeing it since the family moved into the palace. It was as lavish as she expected, with a bed just as large as mama and baba's. The walls were draped with woven rugs and a chest of drawers stood nearby the bed. She walked to the chest of drawers and opened it. As she suspected it was filled with beautiful clothing befitting the Bene's daughter. Any other time she would be eager to take out each outfit and try them on, but not this night. She was tired, embarrassed, and overwhelmed. Someone tapped on her door, and she went to open it. An older woman stood at the door holding a water basin with towels draped over her shoulder.

"Your wash water," the woman said. "If you wish I can draw you a full bath."

"Thank you." Omolewa reached for the basin, but the woman pulled it away.

"I will bring it inside, mamoyo," she said.

Omolewa trailed the woman to the basin pedestal.

"What is your name?" she asked.

"Aizivaishe," the woman said.

"Are you my new servant?"

"For now," the woman answered.

Aizivaishe placed the basin in the pedestal then put the towels beside it.

"Thank you," Omolewa said.

"You don't have to thank me," the woman replied. "I will wait until you are finished."

Omolewa washed up.

"Where is Palesa?" she asked.

"She has been reassigned to the fields," Aizivaishe said.

"Can you tell her I'm sorry for what happened?"

"You should be," Aizivaishe replied. "If it were not for you, she would not be in so much trouble."

Aizivaishe's words struck hard. Omolewa turned to look at the woman and saw the anger in her eyes despite her subservient pose.

"I only wanted to get away for a while," Omolewa said. "I did not know it would cause so much trouble."

"Of course, you did not know *mutora*," the woman said.

Omolewa did not know what *mutora* meant, but she was sure by the tone in Aizivaishe's voice it was an insult.

"That will be all," she said.

"Are you sure, mamoyo?" The woman's tone was condescending.

"Yes, I'm absolutely sure," Omolewa replied. "I will inform the Bene of your assistance."

"I'm sure you will," Aizivaishe replied.

The woman marched out of the room, slamming the door behind her.

Omolewa's shoulders slumped as she climbed into the bed. She would say nothing to the Bene about Aizivaishe's rude behavior. She had caused enough trouble for one day. Tomorrow she would do exactly as she was told, and she would find a way to make things up to Palesa. Until then she would try to sleep and forget the day.

- 7 -

The day began as usual, breakfast with her family, the Bene, Kashta and the others. She followed Kashta to the training room, her mood still pensive from the day before. To her surprise Kulal was waiting for both of them.

"I asked Kulal to come today," Kashta said. "After yesterday's incident I decided we need to lighten the mood."

Omolewa was suddenly curious. "How will we do that?"

"We'll play catch," Kulal replied.

A medium sized ball rested at his feet. Without looking at it or touching it Kulal lifted the ball to his chest height. Moments later it came streaking at Omolewa. She raised her arms before her for protection then braced herself for the impact. Instead, the ball fell at her feet. She looked at Kulal and he laughed.

"Sorry," he said. "I couldn't help it."

"You're as bad as Diwani, only bigger," she said.

Kashta and Kulal laughed, forcing Omolewa to smile.

"So, I guess I must lift this ball then pass it back to Kulal," she said.

"Correct," Kashta replied. "I know you have the ability. But like before we work on precision and control."

Omolewa looked at the ball, concentrating her ashé. It lifted from the floor to her hands.

"I'm ready," Kulal said.

She extended her arms and the ball drifted to her brother. He folded his arms and tapped his foot as it came to him, finally resting inches away from his face before falling hard. Kulal jumped back as the ball barely missed his toes.

"Hey!" he shouted.

Omolewa smirked. "Sorry."

Kulal smirked back. "You learn fast."

"Okay now," Kashta said. "Enough mischief. Pass the ball back and forth. Omolewa try your best not to use gestures. They give away your intentions."

"Yes, Kashta," she replied.

Omolewa and Kulal passed the ball back and forth the entire morning. As siblings are wont to do, they moved about the room, trying their best to make it difficult for the other to catch the ball and pass it back. Kashta sat out of range of the exchange, shouting words of instruction to Omolewa. She was gesturing less but still needed to do so by the time the session ended. As before she felt physically tired, and a slight headache appeared at the base of her head. She was relieved when she saw a servant enter the room with a bowl of upenya fruit.

"You did well," Kashta said. "Your control is rapidly improving. I think we will be done with manipulation training sooner than I planned."

Omolewa chewed the sweet fruit, her strength replenishing as she talked.

"What will be next?" she asked.

"Formulation," Kulal said. "That will be much more challenging."

"What is formulation?"

Kashta smiled.

"Making something from nothing," he replied.

"That's impossible," Omolewa said.

Kashta smiled. "Exactly!"

Kashta began to pace and gesticulate.

"The world is filled with substances, some we can see, some we can't. This concept must be grasped before any matter manipulation can be achieved."

"Matter manipulation?"

"Yes, Omolewa. Matter manipulation," Kashta replied.

Kulal came and sat by her. He took a big bite of his upenya then talked with his mouth full.

"Why did you get him started?"

"I didn't do anything," Omolewa replied. "I just asked him a question."

"You asked him the wrong question. He'll go on forever about that."

"Don't interrupt me!" Kashta said.

Kulal stood. "And on that note, I must take my leave. I take it you're done with me?"

"For now, *nevanji*," Kashta said.

Kulal leaned closer to Omolewa.

"He must really be angry. He addressed me formally."

Kulal waved as he exited the room.

"I'll meet you after your class," he said. "I'll be your escort until mama finds you a suitable new servant."

Kulal's words made her think of Palesa, and her mood dampened.

Kashta droned on, but Omolewa wasn't listening. All she could think of was Palesa. There was no reason for her to stay because she wasn't listening. Kashta's voice finally faded.

"If that is all for today, I must get to my classes," she said.

"Of course," Kashta said. "We will resume training and teaching tomorrow."

"Since I'm here I'll walk you to your class," Kulal said.

Kulal and Omolewa left the training room and strolled across the courtyard to the palace wall, three guards close behind.

"You never go without guards?" Omolewa asked.

"Never . . . well almost never. There are times that I do need my privacy."

"You don't need them for protection. Your ashé is amazing."

"Thank you," Kulal said as he struck a pompous pose. Omolewa giggled.

"It doesn't matter how strong I am," he said. "These are tense times. It's best not to be caught alone."

"Kashta believes I'll be as strong as you one day," she said.

"You'll be stronger," Kulal said.

"How do you know?"

"Because you are your mother's daughter and my sister," he answered. "You bear the symbol as well."

Omolewa touched her forehead then decided to change the subject to one more urgent.

"Kulal, will Palesa be allowed to serve me again?"

The humor fled Kulal's face, replaced by a grim mask.

"Palesa violated her duties," he said. "I'm sure it was her idea to go to the market for you didn't know it existed. She should be glad mama didn't banish her from the city."

"That is not necessary!" Omolewa blurted.

"Look, Omolewa, it is very important you understand what I'm going to tell you," Kulal said. "Everyone in this realm has a duty, especially when it comes to the palace. Each of us must perform our function in order for the realm to remain strong, even a servant like Palesa. When procedure is not followed there can be terrible consequences."

"It was only a walk to the market, and it was me who insisted on it," Omolewa replied.

"And look what happened," Kulal said. "That is why you must stay protected when you are outside the palace walls."

"I understand," Omolewa said. She was getting annoyed by Kulal. "But still, this is not Palesa's fault."

"Palesa knew better," Kulal said. "She should have at least approached the guards and asked for escort."

"How long will her punishment last?" Omolewa asked.

"As long as the Bene sees fit," Kulal said.

"I see," Omolewa said. Her despondent feeling must have registered somehow to Kulal.

"Look, whatever punishment she endures won't be harsh," he said. "I'll see that it's not."

"Won't you be defying the Bene?"

"It won't be the first time," he said. "And it's only you and me. You can call her mama."

"I'm not quite ready to do that," Omolewa said "I need more time."

They stopped before the entrance to the academy.

"Take all the time you need," he said. "But at some point, it will come up in conversation. I hope the two of you will be alone when it does."

Panya decided to ask Kulal another question that had been on her mind.

"Aizivaishe called me a *mutora*," she said. "What does that mean?"

"Damn that woman!" Kulal said. "Mutora means foreigner. There was a time when Zimbabwa kept itself isolated from the rest of Ki Khanga. Calling a person mutora was considered an insult."

"If I told the Bene what she said will she be punished?" Omolewa asked.

"Aizivaishe is a special case," Kulal replied. "She has served mama since she was a child. They were practically raised together. She is known for speaking her mind and getting away with it. I will say something to mama about it, but don't expect anything to happen, especially in public."

"Don't say anything. I don't wish to get anyone else in trouble," Omolewa said. "I just need to know if I need to be careful around her."

"Aizivaishe is not your enemy. It takes time for her to warm up to people. Soon she will love you as I do."

Omolewa stopped walking. Kulal's words caught her off guard.

"Do you love me Kulal?"

Kulal shared with her the warmest smile.

"Of course, I do. You're my sister."

Omolewa entered the classroom then took her seat, thinking about Kulal's words. His emotions seemed genuine; she only wished she felt the same for him and the Bene. Although she was far from making any fateful decisions, she decided that she would never challenge Kulal for Bene, even if her ashé became stronger. She did not want the honor, or the position and she doubted she ever would.

There was no reciting for class; the mudzidzisi drilled them on the concepts she'd introduced the day before. Omolewa had no problem with the work; she enjoyed numbers and calculations. The work took her mind off Palesa for a time, but as soon as class was over, she began thinking about the girl again. Although she was her servant for only a brief time Omolewa realized that she saw Palesa as a friend. She would have to say something to the Bene about this. She would no longer remain silent.

Mudiwa approached her as cleaned her tablet.

"Where is Palesa?" she asked.

"She will not be coming anymore," Omolewa said.

"Oh, I see. Maybe you can continue the lessons with her?"

"No. That won't be possible."

Omolewa hurried from the room before Mudiwa asked any more questions. Kulal was waiting for her as he promised.

"And how was your class?" he asked.

"It was good. We worked on more mathematics today."

Kulal drew in his lips then shook his head. Omolewa laughed.

"Is there anything you like about learning?" she asked him.

"The best thing about class is when it's over," he replied.

"You don't mean that."

"Yes, I do. With all my heart."

"But Kashta said the more you know the stronger your ashé."

"Which is why I'll never be as strong as you, Lewa."

Kulal grasped her arm.

"Come go to the market with me."

Omolewa frowned. "I don't want to."

"Don't blame the market for what happened," he said. "It will be fine. Number one, you're with me. Number two, we have bodyguards. Number three, you're with me. Do you know what number four will be?"

Omolewa grinned. "I guess it has something to do with you."

"Of course! Now let's go."

They strolled to the market. As Kulal said it was a much different experience visiting as the daughter of the Bene. The gate guards made an elaborate display of recognition as they entered, those surrounding them prostrating. They were immediately set upon by the merchants, women and men jostling about to offer them their various wares. The guards kept them at a reasonable distance as Kulal inspected each offering and shared a jovial comment. Omolewa watched him in fascination. He was a natural charmer, always knowing what to say and how to say it. There was sincerity in his voice that each person he spoke to seem to feel. They would look at him pleasantly after he spoke to them, some whispering to each other as they smiled.

"Mukoma!"

Kulal smiled as he looked beyond the ring of merchants.

"Munin'ina!" he shouted back.

The crowd parted and a boy stepped forward. Omolewa held back a gasp. It was the same boy that pursued her and Palesa the day before.

"That's him!" she said to Kulal.

"What do you mean?"

"That's the boy that chased me and Palesa yesterday!" Kulal pointed at the boy.

"Him?" he laughed. "He's the last person you should have run from."

The guards let the boy through and Kulal hugged him.

"Tatonga! It's been a long time!"

"Yes, it has, Kulal," the boy replied. "We have missed you."

"And we have missed you. When did your family return?"

"Two weeks ago," Tatonga replied.

"And you have not come to the palace?" Kulal made a face. "The Bene will not be happy when she hears this."

"She will be happy when she sees what mama brought her. Our time in Wadantu was very fruitful."

Tatonga turned his attention to Omolewa, and she looked away embarrassed.

"Is this the long-lost sister?" he asked.

"Yes," Kulal replied. "Omolewa has come home. Well, I went and fetched her home."

Tatonga suddenly prostrated before her, catching her off guard.

"I honor you, *mamoyo* Omolewa," he said. "It is a blessing from Eda to have you home once again."

"She said you frightened her and her servant at the market yesterday," Kulal said. "I was hoping you would grow up to be less ugly."

Tatonga laughed as he came to his feet. "I must apologize. We had heard the good news and when I saw you with your servant, I assumed it was you. I should have approached you more cautiously."

Kulal put his arm around Tatonga's shoulders.

"Tatonga's family is close friends of ours and has been for many years. They are merchants by trade and spend much time out of the country. It's good to have them back."

"It is good to meet you formally Tatonga," Omolewa said. "If I had known who you were I would not have screamed as loud."

Tatonga and Kulal laughed.

"She is definitely your sister," Tatonga said. "May we join you?"

"Of course!" Kulal said.

Tatonga fell in beside Kulal on his left, Omolewa on his right. He wrapped his arms around both them and strode through the market. He seemed to no longer be interested in the wares surrounding him, and neither was Omolewa. She listened to the two of them talk of old and new things as she stole glances at Tatonga. He was tall, almost as tall as Kulal, but definitely younger. He possessed the same ebony hue of most Zimbabwans with light brown eyes that seemed to sparkle from within. When he smiled his cheeks dimpled. There was a slight scar under his right eye; whether it was from an injury or scarification she could not tell. What she could tell was that he was a handsome boy, and from what she'd seen so far, a boy with a warm personality. But she would reserve her opinion until after she knew him better, which from how Kulal enjoyed his company she would have plenty of opportunity to do so.

Omolewa didn't realize they had left the market until they were far away. They ambled through the streets of the central district, the part of the city surrounding the palace and filled with the compounds of Zimbabwans of lineage and wealthy foreigners.

"So, you grew up in Nacala?" Tatonga asked.

His question caught her off-guard.

"Ah…yes I did. You know the city?"

"I have heard of it but have never visited," Tatonga replied. "I've recently passed initiation rites and now travel with my mother or father on their merchant journeys. Wadantu was my first. It is a beautiful land, but not as beautiful as the Kiswala Islands. At least that is what I am told."

Tatonga's words made her miss home.

"Yes, Nacala is beautiful," she replied.

"I'm sure you miss it."

"I do. Very much. I miss the palm trees most, how they sway with the winds."

"Zimbabwa is a beautiful land as well." Tatonga turned to Kulal. "Have you taken her to the mountains yet?"

"No, I haven't," Kulal replied. "But I plan to."

"You should go to the mountains," Tatonga said. "It is the most beautiful part of Zimbabwa. The air is pure and temperate, and the nights cool and relaxing. You would love it there."

"She is in studies for now," Kulal said. "But when Kashta allows I will take her. As a matter of fact, you should come with us!"

A sly grin came to Tatonga's face. "And I'm sure Shamiso is invited as well."

"That would be rather obvious, wouldn't it?" Kulal replied.

"Shamiso is my older sister," Tatonga said to Omolewa. "Kulal has been in love with her since before he was born."

"Before Daarila struck Ki Khanga with his Axe," Kulal added. "Maybe I can persuade mama to move to the dry season palace. We are overdue."

Omolewa eyes widened.

"The dry season palace? The Bene has another palace?"

"We have three palaces," Kulal said. "Maputo is where we spend most of our time. Then there is the mountain palace where we spend the dry season and the coastal palace where we reside during the end of the merchant season."

They halted before a large compound; its high white walls festooned with intricately drawn patterns.

"This is our compound," Tatonga said. "Somehow I knew we would end up here."

"What can I say?" Kulal replied. "The heart wants what it wants. Who am I to get in its way?"

The guards standing outside the gate prostrated before Kulal and Omolewa before opening the thick wooden gate, revealing a courtyard very different from that of the palace. It was filled with people, animals, and merchandise.

"This is like a marketplace," Omolewa remarked.

"It's always like this when we've returned from a journey," Tatonga said. "Tomorrow we will begin distribution. Some will go to other compounds nearby and others will go to the Bene's market. When I was younger this was the most exciting time. I would play with my brothers and sisters in the confusion and try not to get killed."

"You call that fun?" Omolewa frowned.

"It was to a child," he replied.

An older man emerged from the confusion, dressed in a shimmering blue *tobe* that cascaded over his pants and brushed his sandaled feet. The cap on his head matched the robe. He shared an easy smile with the three of them then bowed deeply.

"Forgive me if I do not prostrate before you," he said. "It is a long journey both ways for an old man such as I."

"An unnecessary one as well," Kulal replied. "Hello, uncle."

"Hello, Kulal."

Kulal and the old man embraced. Tatonga hugged the man as well before turning toward Omolewa.

"Baba, this is . . ."

"I know who she is," the old man said. "It is wonderful to see you home, Omolewa. You have inherited your mother's beauty. I'm sure you have inherited her talents as well."

The elder extended his arms and Omolewa hugged him. As she touched him an odd feeling passed through her, a feeling that made her uncomfortable. She pulled away as quickly as she could.

"It is nice to meet you . . . uncle," she said.

The man smiled. "I was present at your birth," he said. "It was a joyous and sad affair. Those were difficult times. Your mother persevered, as did we all. Now you are back. I know she is extremely happy."

"We all are," Kulal said.

"Tell me, how does your father fair?"

"He is well," Omolewa said. "He is here with me."

The old man's smile dampened. "Is he?"

"Yes," she replied. "As is my mama, brother and sister."

"Ah, a true family reunion," the old man said. He turned and waved his hand.

"As you can see, we have much to do, so you will excuse me if I do not entertain you further. Things would go much smoother if some of us spent as much time at home helping as they did dallying in the market."

Omolewa followed Kulal as he inspected some of the merchandise. He stopped then picked up a wooden staff crowned with what looked like a man with the head of a hawk.

"What is this?" Kulal asked. "I've never seen anything like this."

"And I doubt you ever will," Tatonga's baba said. He took the staff from Kulal. "It's a talisman staff from Menu-Kash."

Kulal's eyes went wide. "You went there? How was that possible?"

"A merchant never tells his secrets," Tatonga's baba replied. "This item will fetch me a nice profit from the right person."

"The Bene would be interested in that, I think," Tatonga said.

"I have items more interesting for the Bene," his father said.

"But this is unique," Tatonga replied.

The old man cut his eyes at Tatonga. The boy frowned.

"It seems I've been called to work," he said. "When will we visit the palace, baba?"

"That is for your mother to decide," the old man said. "I'm just an old merchant. I do what I'm told when it comes to these formal things."

Kulal cleared his throat. "Uncle, is Shamiso here?"

The old man grinned then walked away. Kulal's face dropped and Omolewa laughed.

"You look like Pik-Pik when he's hungry."

Moments later a tall, graceful woman emerged from the confusion, draped in a golden kanga that fell from her shoulders to her feet. Her matching headwrap rose from her head like a crown, her beaded necklaces and jeweled bracelets rattling to the rhythm of her gait. She smiled at Kulal demurely then turned her attention to Omolewa.

"Hello little munin'ina," she said. Her voice was mature, like a woman beyond her years.

"Hello, Shamiso," Omolewa said.

Shamiso then looked into Kulal's eyes the smiled. "Hello Kulal."

"It is as if the sun rises before me," he replied.

Tatonga rolled his eyes. "I hope this doesn't last long."

"It won't," Shamiso said. "I come only to greet you. There is much for the both of us to do. Mama sent me."

Tatonga laughed. "Baba just told me I am needed. We know why you are here."

"Go away," Shamiso said.

Tatonga waved at Omolewa. "We will visit soon. I would love to hear more about Nacala."

Omolewa felt a warm rush in her cheeks.

"I would be happy to tell you."

Tatonga grinned. "Good!"

He bounced away to the house. When Omolewa looked about Kulal and Shamiso were holding hands.

"I will see you soon as well," he said.

"I hope so," she replied. "It has been a long time."

"I'm too young to be a chaperone," Omolewa said.

The two laughed as they let go of each other's hands.

"I guess some things are the same in Nacala as they are in Maputo," Shamiso said. "We will visit soon. I'm looking forward getting to know you, little munin'ina."

Shamiso turned then walked away, stealing one last glance at Kulal. Kulal stared back, a dream-like smile on his face. Omolewa tugged his shirt to break his trance.

"Come on lover boy," she said. "Take me home. I'm getting hungry."

Omolewa and Kulal strolled back to the palace. Kulal talked of Shamiso the entire time, but Omolewa barely listened. She kept thinking about Shamiso's father. There was something odd about him. At first glance he seemed like any other successful man, but when he touched her Omolewa sensed otherwise. This had something to do with her ashé she was sure. She would have to ask Kashta about this at their next session.

Kulal and Omolewa parted ways once they reached the palace. She went immediately to her parents' room. Diwani and Kazija greeted her with their usual enthusiasm, and once again Pik-Pik seemed relieved to see her, jumping onto her kanga and scrambling into her arms. Mama and baba smiled, their emotions more subdued than normal. Something was going on. She sat at the table before their bed and they joined her.

"How was your day?" mama asked.

"It was busy as always," she replied. "I trained with Kulal today. Kashta said we will begin working with formulations soon."

"Formulations?" baba said. "That's serious business."

Omolewa was surprised by baba's comments.

"You know of formulations?"

"Yes," he said. "When I served as a Mikijen we protected quite a few sonchai employed by the Wakuu. They would use their ashé to create amazing things. Does Kashta believe you have the talent to do the same?"

"I don't know," she said. "I must learn the concepts before I can attempt it. He says the more I know the more powerful I will be."

Baba's look went solemn, as did mama's.

"Is there something wrong?" she asked.

"No," mama said. "Baba and I are making plans to return to work."

"Why?" Omolewa asked.

"People were not meant to be idle," mama answered. "Eda gave us our talents in order to strive. Even the Bene has duties she must attend to, and so do we."

"What will you do?"

"I am going back into service," baba said. "The Bene has asked me to train her new warriors and guards."

"And I will weave again," mama said. "It will be easier not having to prepare meals and constantly chase your brother and sister."

"That used to be my job," Omolewa said with a smile.

"You should chase me now!" Diwani said.

"Me too!" Kazija chimed in.

Omolewa placed Pik-Pik on the floor.

"Not today," she said. "I'm too tired."

She sprang from her seat and grabbed Kazija. Kazija screamed in glee and Diwani ran away.

"Chase me! Chase me!"

Omolewa tucked Kazija under her arm then pursued Diwani around the room with Pik-Pik prancing around her feet. She placed Kazija on the floor then scooped up Diwani, her brother wiggling to escape her grip. She threw him over her shoulder like a squirming bag of sorghum then chased Kazija, who laughed and stumbled about. They went back and forth until all three were totally exhausted, lying on the floor in a giggling pile.

There was a knock on the door.

"Enter," Baba said.

A servant stuck in his head. He gave Omolewa and her siblings a disapproving glance before turning his attention to mama and baba.

"The evening meal is ready," he said. "The Bene is expecting you."

"Tell the Bene we will not be able to make the evening meal," she said. "We will like to have our meal in our room."

The servant looked stunned.

"But . . . but the Bene requested it!"

"Did she insist?" mama asked.

"No."

"Then I'm sure she will understand," mama said. "Please relay our message and arrange for our meals to be brought here."

"Ah . . . yes. I will do so."

The servant left the room quickly. Omolewa and baba looked at mama with worried faces.

"Was that wise?" baba said.

"We'll soon find out," mama replied. "We need some time to ourselves. I'll be so happy once we find a house."

Baba shrugged. "I will, too. I miss the privacy."

"I wish we could go back to Nacala," Omolewa said.

"Me too!" Diwani said.

"Me too!" Kazija shouted.

Pik-Pik let out a loud bark.

"He said, 'me too!'" Diwani said.

Servants appeared later with the meal, carrying a large table on which to serve them.

"We will not need that," mama said. "Can you bring us a rug instead?"

The servants looked at each other with annoyed expressions.

"Yes aunt," one of them said.

A servant hurried away then returned with a rolled rug under his arm. He unrolled it before the foot of the bed. It was worn and frayed, obviously meant to be an insult but was anything but.

"Perfect!" mama said.

The other servants placed the bowls of food on the rug then went about their duties. The family gathered around the meal then ate, chatting and laughing. Omolewa fed pieces of her meal to Pik-Pik, the little ferret chattering away as well. They were almost done with their meal when the door swung wide and Hajanika entered.

"The Bene comes," she announced.

Omolewa and the others stood as the Bene entered. She waved them down before they could prostrate before her, sharing a generous smile as she approached.

"You are family," she said. "There is no need for you to prostrate. I am however disappointed that you did not invite me to share your meal."

"My apologies," mama said. "I felt we needed some informal time together."

"I understand," she said, then shocked everyone when she sat on the floor before them.

"Bene!" Hajanika exclaimed.

"You will not remember this," the Bene replied.

"No Bene, I will not."

Hajanika bowed, a cross look on her face as she exited the room.

"I know this transition is difficult," the Bene said. "I want you to know that our acceptance of you as family is sincere. I know that our lives can seem restricted to those not used to it and there is no remedy for it. It is true, we have certain rules to follow and responsibilities to uphold. It is the price that we pay in exchange for being favored by Eda and the ancestors to lead our people."

She picked up a portion of bread then nibbled on it. Pik-Pik appeared at her side, rising up on her hind legs. The Bene smiled.

"Are you hungry?"

"No, she's just greedy," Omolewa replied.

The Bene tore a piece of bread then fed it to the ferret, gazing at Omolewa as she did so.

"Aunt, I would like to talk to Omolewa after dinner," she said. "Would that be possible?"

"You don't have to ask permission," mama said. "You're the Bene."

"Yes, I must," the Bene said. "We are family, and I must respect you as her mother."

Mama and baba shared surprised glances.

"Yes, you may speak with her," mama said.

"Thank you." Pik-Pik rubbed against the Bene's leg, and she responded by massaging her neck.

"Are you ready Lewa?" she asked.

A nervous chill ran down Omolewa's spine.

"Yes. I am ready."

The Bene picked up Pik-Pik then stood. The ferret was at ease with the Bene, as relaxed as it was with Omolewa. That was a good thing, Omolewa thought.

They left the room together and were greeted by Hajanika.

"We will walk alone," the Bene said.

Hajanika bowed then walked away. The Bene waited until Hajanika disappeared around a corner before sighing.

"Hajanika is a good djele," she said. "But her constant hovering can be quite exasperating."

"Why does she do so?" Omolewa asked.

"It is her duty to record my history so that no one forgets me," the Bene said. "She is very good at what she does, but I don't think everything about me should be remembered."

The Bene walked and Omolewa followed.

"How was your walk today?"

"It was good," Omolewa said. "Kulal is very nice to me."

"Kulal loves you very much. He missed you so much when we sent you away. He spoke of bringing you home every day."

"I still can't think of Zimbabwa as home," Omolewa confessed. "That word brings memories of Nacala."

"Nacala will always be first for you," Omolewa said. "As will your mama and baba."

The Bene fell silent for a moment then stopped walking. Omolewa felt her hand on her shoulder and was swept with that same sensation of odd familiarity.

"Omolewa," she said.

Omolewa turned to look at the Zimbabwa ruler, her mother. She could see and feel the pain in the woman's eyes which made it so uncomfortable to be in her presence.

"I know I have no right to ask this of you, but I would like it if you thought of me as your mother as well."

Omolewa turned away then continued walking, unnerved by the Bene's request.

"It is a strange thing," she finally said. "I look at you and I see myself. I know you are my mother, and yet…"

"I did not raise you," the Bene said. "The love a child has for its mother grows over the years, but the love a mother has for her child begins the moment we know you are inside us. I know it's not fair for me to say this, but I hope that one day you will love me as I love you."

"I will try," Omolewa said. She didn't know what else to say.

"That is all I can ask," the Bene said.

They reached the atrium. The Bene sauntered to her favorite bench and sat; Omolewa sat beside her.

"I'm told you met Tatonga," she said.

"I did," Omolewa said as she smiled. "He is a pleasant boy and Kulal is fond of him."

"Kulal is easy to like. But there is much more to that meeting."

"I know. Kulal is in love with Tatonga's sister."

The Bene smiled. "It is good that they love each other. It will make their marriage easier to bear."

"Marriage? I didn't know it was that serious."

"Kulal and Shamiso's marriage was arranged before they were born," the Bene said. "The Iekanjika clan is one of high lineage, one whose family has produced a number of Benes. Kulal and Shamiso's marriage will solidify the alliance between our families."

"I have heard how those of high standing arrange such things," she said. "It is not so for people like me."

"You are of high lineage," the Bene said.

Omolewa did not like the direction the conversation was heading. She now knew why the Bene had asked her about Tatonga.

"I'm not ready for marriage, especially to someone I barely know," she said.

The Bene's eyes widened. "You waste no time getting to the point."

"I did not ask to come here," Omolewa said. "I understand what is happening and I am doing what is required of me. But there are some things I will not agree with. I will not be told who I am to marry, if I choose to marry at all."

The Bene's face took on a stern countenance. Omolewa worried if she had gone too far. She was always one to speak her mind when she disagreed, but this was not mama or baba sitting beside here. This was the ruler of Zimbabwa, a powerful woman who was used to getting her way. She was also her mother.

"We will speak of this some other time," she finally said. "Let's return to the others."

Their walk back to her parents' room was uncomfortable. The Bene unexpectedly kissed her cheek before she entered the room.

"You don't realize how much you are like me," she said. "That is a good and a bad thing. "Goodnight, daughter.""

Mama and the others were gathered around the rug. Instead of everyone listening to baba tell one of his stories of faraway lands; it was Diwani who took the floor. Omolewa was smiling before she heard his words.

"And then the big bird told the ant, 'I would eat you but you are so small it would only make me hungrier. Then the ant told the bird, 'If you ate me, I would make your stomach hurt so bad you would never eat anything again!'"

Mama and baba looked up to see her.

"How was your walk?" mama asked.

"Hey!" Diwani said. "I'm telling my story!"

"That's enough for the night," baba said. "It's time to sleep."

Diwani rolled his eyes then fell onto his back. Kazija did the same.

Baba took the two over to their beds while Omolewa sat down with mama.

"So, how did it go?"

Omolewa looked into her mother's eyes then sighed.

"She wanted to talk about marriage."

"What?" Mama's face looked angry. "Why would she want to do that?"

"I met a boy today," Omolewa replied. "His name is Tatonga, and his family is very powerful. Kulal is expected to marry his sister, Shamiso."

"What does that have to do with you?" mama said.

"I don't know, but I think the Bene expects me to marry someone like Tatonga one day in order to strengthen their bonds with the other families."

"By Eda's hands," mama said. "I will not allow it!"

Baba came over to them, concerned.

"What is this? What is going on?"

"The Bene is trying to arrange a marriage for Lewa!" mama said.

"No mama, I'm not sure," Omolewa said

"No!" baba said. "She goes too far!"

Omolewa regretted sharing the information. Mama and baba were furious.

"We will talk to her tomorrow as first light," mama said. "She should not make such decisions without us. I know we are not your true parents, but you are our child in every other way."

"Exactly," baba said.

Omolewa looked at both of her parents. Beneath their anger she sensed another emotion, desperation. Both seemed to be avoiding what she knew was true.

"She is the Bene," Omolewa said. "And I am her daughter. If she decided that this will happen, what can we do to stop it?"

Mama and baba anger subsided.

"Nothing," mama finally said.

"No, there is something we can do," baba said, still defiant. "We can go back to Nacala."

"They found us in Nacala after all these years," mama said.

"Then we will go to Sati-Baa," baba replied. "It is a huge city and easy to get lost in. Or…"

"Or what?" mama said.

"We can go to the East," he said. "It would take some time to arrange, but it can be done. However, once we go, we cannot come back."

Omolewa had only seen her parents look helpless once, and that was when the kidnappers broke into their house, and they were rescued by Kulal. This time there would be no rescue.

"There is nothing we can do about it tonight," mama finally said. "Let's all try to get some sleep. We will need our energy for the morning."

Baba nodded. "Don't worry Lewa. We will sort this out."

"I know baba," she said. "I am not worried."

She spent the night with the family, but she did not sleep. The Bene's revelation was far beyond anything she had imagined. Mama and baba would try to have their say, but they would fail. Though the Bene's demeanor was pleasant, there was hardness behind her words. She thought of what the Bene told her about her brothers as well as what the servant Aizivaishe accused the Bene of. If mama and baba defied her, they might be hurt or killed. She would have to figure a way out of this mess. She rolled onto her left said and prevented tears from staining her cheeks. Her blessing was becoming a cage.

- 8 -

Tension was high at the morning meal. Mama and baba sat side by side, glaring at the Bene. Kashta's eyes wandered, a concerned look on his face. Kulal was jovial as always, yet there was stiffness in his movements that revealed his unease. Hajanika observed them all, recording the moment as was her duty. Only the Bene seemed unaffected as she filled her plate with the foods on the platter. Omolewa was rigid, waiting for the argument to begin.

"What is this about Lewa getting married?" mama said.

The Bene froze then placed her bread on her plate. She gave Omolewa scolding look before turning her attention to mama.

"No marriage is being planned for Omolewa . . . yet," she said. "I was just discussing with her the responsibilities of her position."

"What position?" baba asked.

The Bene's expression became hard. She pushed away from the table then stood, taking on a regal bearing. Kulal's face became serious as well as he looked to his mother.

"What do you think has been going on these few months?" she asked. "Why do you think Kulal was sent to bring Omolewa back? Do you think this is some game you will play until you're tired and ready to go back to your meager lives in Nacala?"

She looked at baba then scowled.

"You were given a mission Mikijen," she said, using baba's old profession to describe him. "And you were paid well for it. Apparently, you lost sight of your duty."

Baba looked at mama then looked away. Mama's eyes went wide.

"I am sorry that he did not explain everything to you, and I am sorry that you feel you have some say over what Omolewa's future will be. She should have been raised knowing what would someday be. Instead, you lived a lie."

"How could I know what to tell her!" Baba blurted. "You blocked my memory!"

"You knew enough," the Bene replied. "The rest we blocked to keep you from revealing the truth in case those who sought her found her before we were ready."

"But I don't want to marry!" Omolewa said.

"And you won't for now," the Bene said. "Any such thing is far away at this point. You have your education and training to concentrate on. I'm sorry I brought up the subject. I thought you were mature enough to handle the discussion. Apparently, I was wrong."

The Bene looked to one of the servants.

"I will finish my meal in my room. The others can do what they please."

The Bene marched from the room, Hajanika close behind. Everyone else sat still for a time, looking at each other with bewildered expressions.

"She's angry," Diwani said.

Omolewa smiled at her brother then patted his head.

"Yes, she is. Now finish your food."

They completed their meal in silence. Kulal was the first to finish. He stood then attempted to smile.

"Not the way I planned to start my day," he said. The humor was lost on the others.

"I apologize for the Bene," he continued. "These have not been good days for her. There is so much that she cannot tell you, at least not now. But you must realize that life has changed for you all. It will never be the way it was. I'm sorry."

Kulal hurried from the room. Omolewa looked to Kashta, anticipating the Kamite to explain. Instead, he stood then walked toward the door.

"I expect you to be on time for your training, Omole-wa," he said.

"I will," she replied.

Kashta left the room. Omolewa looked at mama and baba. Baba looked sad, but mama was angry.

"She thinks this is over, but it's not," she said.

Baba placed a hand on mama's shoulder, and she brushed it away.

"You accept all this?" she asked.

"The Bene has not told a lie," he replied. He placed his hand over mama's and this time she did not rebuff him. He then looked into Omolewa's eyes with an expression that brought tears to her eyes.

"This is our life now," he said. "This is what it was intended to be. We let ourselves believe it would be different, but it would always come to this. We must be strong now for each other and especially for you, Lewa. Embrace what has been given to you. Accept your place in this family. You are our daughter, but you are her child."

Omolewa shook as baba uttered those last words. He was right. She had thought there was some way to deny her new responsibilities, but the only way that would happen was if the Bene decided to release her from her obligation and that was not to be. Her life had been determined long before she was born.

She stood. "I must go to my classes."

Mama looked at her, tears at the corners of her eyes.

"We will see you soon," she said.

Omolewa didn't reply. She walked alone to the training room. Kashta and Kulal were there to meet her, both men subdued. It was Kulal who spoke first.

"It's not so bad," he said.

Omolewa was in no mood for his sympathy. She looked at Kashta.

"Can we begin?"

The sage cleared his throat. "Yes. Today we will concentrate on dexterity."

He placed three balls before Omolewa of the same size.

"Manipulations of several objects will fine tune your skills," he said. "The more you can handle, the better your control."

"Like the jugglers in the market," she answered.

Kashta grinned. "Exactly. Today we will work on simple tasks, like lifting them and moving them about."

Omolewa closed her eyes for a moment to summon her ashé. When she opened them, she lifted the balls hovered before her.

"I am ready," she said.

"Yes, you are," Kashta replied.

"She did that too easy," Kulal said, a hint of jealousy in his voice.

"Interesting," Kashta said.

Omolewa maneuvered the balls as she had seen the jugglers do. This was easier because she didn't have to catch them. She smiled as she looked at Kashta and Kulal, but the two men looked back at her with stunned expressions. Omolewa's smiled faded.

"Am I doing something wrong?" she asked.

"No," Kashta replied.

"You're doing quite well," Kulal said.

"I guess there is no need to ask you to do the first task," Kashta said. "You're well beyond that. Something tells me you have used your skills more that you revealed."

Omolewa lowered the balls to the floor.

"Sometimes mama needed things lifted and moved when baba was not home," she said. "So, I did it for her. Well, not exactly."

"What do you mean by that?" Kashta asked.

Omolewa gave a mischievous smile. "Let's just say that mama is not as strong as she thinks she is."

Kulal laughed. "You are definitely my sister."

"Well since manipulation seems to be an advanced skill, let's move on to more challenging tasks."

Kashta pointed out three different platforms in the training room.

"Pick up the balls as you did before then place them on the different surfaces."

Omolewa lifted the balls then began moving them toward the first surface.

"No," Kashta said. "Place each one on a different surface . . . at the same time."

Kulal's eyes widened. "You never asked me to do that."

"Be quiet, Kulal," Kashta said.

Kulal pouted and Omolewa laughed, breaking her concentration. The balls fell to the floor and Kashta gave her a disapproving stare.

"I'm sorry," she said.

Kashta glared at Kulal.

"Begging your pardon *nevanji*, Omolewa needs to concentrate."

"Oh yes, of course," Kulal said. "I'll leave you to it."

Kulal exited the training room. Kashta nodded to Omolewa to resume.

Omolewa lifted the balls again and attempted what Kashta asked. As she tried to move the balls, they all crashed to the floor again. She raised them again and the same thing happened.

"This is impossible!" she said.

"For most, yes," Kashta replied. "But for you, no."

"How do you know?" she said. "You're guessing I can do it. You don't really know."

Kashta came to her.

"I have trained many people with the powers you possess," he said. "But I have never trained anyone with your potential. The fact that you discovered and manipulated your ashé without training is fascinating enough. The fact that you have developed it at such a high level on your own is equally amazing. So, I will push you in ways that I have never done with anyone before. I will ask you to do things that I have not asked anyone else."

"And what if I fail?" Omolewa asked.

"Failure is progress," he said. "With every failure comes knowledge. Besides, if you develop your abilities to where I believe they can be, you will finally have the freedom you seek."

Kashta gave her a knowing look.

"How powerful can I be?" she asked.

"Stronger than me," he replied. "Stronger than the Bene."

"That is why you asked Kulal to leave," she said.

Kashta smiled and new energy swept through Omolewa.

"I want to try again," she said.

Omolewa attempted the manipulation throughout the session but didn't succeed. Normally she would be frustrated, but Kashta's words gave her determination far beyond normal. His words also gave her a bit of caution. She would ask him not to allow Kulal to her training sessions. She had a feeling he was reporting her progress to the Bene and that might not be a wise thing. The Bene had fought her own brothers for control of Zimbabwa; according to Aizivaishe she had killed her husband as well. So how would she feel if the daughter she barely knew began to show powers that were beyond her own? Yes, she would be careful from now on. She would not show what she possessed until she was ready.

Omolewa was exhausted as she trudged to her classes. She kept pace as well as she could but overall, it was a bad day. She was anxious to learn what Kashta had to teach but she would have to pace herself or give up the classes all together to master her ashé. If given the choice she would choose ashé training, but she doubted she would be given the choice.

As she exited the class, she saw a person she didn't expect to see. Tatonga stood across the road, wearing a turquoise silk robe across his torso that fell to his sandaled feet, his left shoulder bare. A bodyguard stood beside him, holding her spear with her right hand as her left hand rested on the hilt of her sword, her stoic face in contrast to Tatonga's easy smile.

"Greetings, Omolewa!" he said. "Kulal told me I would find you here."

"He shouldn't have," Omolewa replied, half joking.

"If my presence disturbs you, I will go about my way," he said. "I don't wish to be a bother. I thought we got along good the second time we met. At least you didn't run away."

Omolewa couldn't help but laugh.

"There is a certain way a boy should introduce himself to a girl," she said. "And it's not running up to her like a puppy. Everyone likes puppies. Not everyone likes boys."

Tatonga dropped his shoulders and frowned.

"So, you do not like me?"

"I didn't say that," Omolewa replied. "You know what I mean."

"Yes, I do, and again I apologize. May I walk you to the palace?"

Omolewa nodded and Tatonga skipped to her side.

"You said you missed your home, Nacala I believe. Tell me about it."

"There's not much to tell," Omolewa said. "It's just home."

"One thing I've learned in my short time traveling is that what is normal to you may be special to someone else," Tatonga said. "So, what is normal in Nacala?"

"There is always a breeze," she said. "Sometimes it is just enough to cool your neck on a hot day, but sometimes it's strong enough to ruffle your clothes."

"Merchants call it the traveling winds," Tatonga said. "They change directions with the seasons."

"Yes, they do," Omolewa said. "The dhows set sail in the direction of the winds. They sail either east or west."

"Yes," Tatonga confirmed. "To the west is Ki Khanga, and to the east? Well, no one knows. The Kiswala keep that secret well."

"Yes, they do," Omolewa agreed.

"What a minute! You're Kiswala!"

Omolewa waved her hand. "That means nothing. The Grand Council controls the trade. Only they know of the lands to the east. Baba said select merchants are allowed to sail there, and only Mikijen of Kiswala blood are taken to protect the dhows. There is a rumor that one man not of Kiswala origin was able to take the journey and he returned with an object of great value."

"And who was this man?" Tatonga asked.

Omolewa mouth twisted as she tried to remember the man's name. It popped in her head, and she snapped her fingers.

"Ket! Omari Ket! That was his name. It's said he was from Sati-Baa."

"Now that is a city I would love to see," Tatonga said. "I've heard amazing things about it."

"Me, too."

A young woman carrying a basket of yellow fruit sauntered up to them. The guard cut her off.

"Move along," she said.

"It's okay," Tatonga said. "It's only a girl."

The girl smiled at him.

"Thank you. Would like one? It's a refreshing fruit for such a warm day."

"I'll take two," Tatonga said. He reached into his waist pouch then gave the girl two silver discs. The girl's eyes widened.

"That is too much!" she said.

"Today it is just enough," Tatonga replied. The girl handed the fruit to Tatonga's guard; the woman placed down her spear then took out her dagger. She peeled the fruit then handed it to Tatonga and Omolewa. Omolewa bit into the fruit and moaned. She'd never tasted anything so succulent.

"This is amazing!" she said. "What is it called?"

"Paradise fruit," Tatonga said. "This is particularly good. It grows in the mountains."

They strolled to the palace, enjoying the fruit and small talk. Omolewa had to admit that Tatonga was a pleasant boy and easy to look at, but she was far from the Bene's intentions. She could see that they would be friends, and that at least was comforting and as much as she needed.

"Well, we're here," Tatonga said. "Thank you for allowing me to escort you home."

"Thank you for the company," Omolewa said.

"Tell Kulal I said hello," he added.

"You should tell him yourself."

Tatonga shook his head. "If I see Kulal I will stay here longer than I should. We never have short conversations."

They bid each other farewell and Omolewa went to her own room. Bath water and a change of clothes awaited her, including someone unexpected. Omolewa grinned and was flush with happiness.

"Palesa!"

She ran to the girl and hugged her tight.

"I missed you so much!" she said. "Are you okay?"

"I am, Lewa," she said, her voice just higher than a whisper. The weakness of it stunned Omolewa.

"Are you sure?"

Palesa nodded. "I will be."

Omolewa led Palesa to a chair then made her sit down.

"What did they do to you?" she asked.

"Nothing I did not deserve," she replied.

"Did they beat you?" Omolewa asked, anger tight in her voice.

"No, they did not beat me," she replied.

"Then what did they do?"

"I was sent to the fields," she said. "It was very hard work."

"I'm glad you're back," Omolewa said.

"But not as I was," Palesa said. "I cannot be your friend, Lewa. I know this now. The Bene does not want anyone close to you outside your family. She is concerned about your safety. Very concerned."

"The Bene does not rule my life!" Omolewa said.

"Yes, she does," Palesa replied. "She controls all of our lives. The sooner you understand this, the easier your time here will be."

Omolewa remembered Kashta's words and the message within them. She took a deep breath to calm herself.

"Will you come with me to dinner?" she asked Palesa.

"If you wish it," the girl replied.

"I do."

Omolewa washed up quickly. Palesa followed her to the dining hall, careful to walk behind her instead of beside her as before. Everyone was waiting as she entered; she took a long look at the Bene before sitting beside mama and baba.

"How was your day?" mama asked.

"Very busy," she replied.

"Your mama and I found a house," baba said.

"The Bene is still allowing you to move?" she asked, sarcasm heavy in her voice. Mama and baba's smiles faded.

She felt a bump against her arm then turned to see Diwani with his fist balled.

"Don't be mean, Lee-lee," he said.

Lee-lee was what he called her when he was mad at her. To him it was an insult; to Omolewa it was just cute. She smiled at him despite her mood.

"I'll be what I want, Wani-face," she replied.

He scowled then punched her again.

The servers interrupted their mock fight. Omolewa took her knife then cut into the yam set before her. She put it in her mouth and chewed; an intense pain struck her stomach, and she dropped the knife.

"Omolewa?" mama said.

The pain struck again, this time so deep she fell from her chair. In moments mama, baba and the others hovered over her. She could barely hear their voices through the searing pain.

"What's happening?"

"Do not touch the food!"

"Lewa! Lewa!"

"Send for the healer now!"

The pain grew into a burning brightness which blinded her then flashed away, leaving a heavy darkness in its wake. She felt a weakness that pushed her toward a sleep which she never wished to awake. She settled into its embrace, hoping for the peace it offered. But that was not to be. The darkness shifted then spiraled, easing from an endless void to warming gray tones. A face formed before her, one that she had never seen before yet seemed familiar. It became the countenance of a woman, ebony toned with piercing brown eyes.

"Sit, my daughter," the woman said.

Omolewa did as she was told. She was surrounded by a lush forest; trees that seemed to reach endlessly upward interspersed with shrubs festooned with flowers crowding their branches. Insects and birds danced in the sky about her, each emitting their own luminous aura. Omolewa looked into the eyes of the woman.

"Am I dead?" she asked.

The woman's smile comforted her more than anything she'd ever experienced.

"Yes," Omolewa concluded. "I am dead."

The woman shook her head.

"You almost were. You must be careful from who you accept gifts."

Omolewa was stunned.

"Tatonga did this?"

The woman shook her head again.

"The food vendor," Omolewa said. "It was her."

"She delivered the weapon, yet even she was not aware."

"Was anyone else hurt?" Omolewa asked.

The woman smiled. "You care far more for others than yourself. That is good. It reveals your kind heart. That will be required for you."

The woman took Omolewa into her arms and Omolewa felt as if life embraced her.

"You are special beyond what you know," the woman said. "I can watch over you, but you must be diligent as well. Now you must go back."

"I don't want to," Omolewa said.

"You must," the woman replied. "You have much to do."

The woman let her go and Omolewa stared into her eyes.

"Eda?" she asked.

The woman smiled. "Go," she said. "Remember you have three mothers."

The darkness around her transformed into bright light which disappeared. Omolewa felt her body and she opened her eyes to see mama and baba hovering over her.

"She's awake!" mama exclaimed. "My baby is awake!"

Mama leaned over and embraced her like she was a fragile object. Omolewa felt weaker than ever in her entire life. She tried to lift her arms, but they would not move.

"Be still," she heard an unfamiliar voice say. "You must conserve your strength."

"We almost lost you," mama whispered. She began to cry.

Omolewa opened her mouth to speak but no words came forth.

"Do as the healer orders," baba said. "Don't try to do anything for now. The Creator has brought you back to us."

It was Eda, she thought.

"Please, I must tend to her," the healer said.

Mama moved aside and was replaced by a gray-haired woman with a stern countenance. She held a bowl in her right hand and a small spoon in her left.

"I'm going to place this on your lips," the woman said. "Lick if you can. If you can't just let it sit. It will absorb through your skin."

The woman spread the liquid on her lips and Omolewa managed to lick it. The sweet taste of upenya spread through her mouth then coursed through her body. She was still weak, but not as weak as moment ago.

"Can you take more?" the healer asked.

Omolewa nodded.

The healer passed the bowl to mama, a smile breaking her serious gaze.

"Here. Take care of your daughter. I have other remedies I need to prepare."

Mama placed more upenya paste on her lips and Omolewa licked it away.

"Oh, my baby," she said. "We almost lost you."

Baba came into view again. His face was not pleasant.

"They are searching the city for the person who did this. Tatonga said you bought fruit from a woman on the street. He was sickened as well, but not as bad as you."

"We won't talk about that now," mama said. "She mustn't worry now."

"You're right," baba said. "I'm just so angry."

Omolewa took a few more spoonfuls then fell into a dreamless sleep. When she awoke, she felt strong enough to sit up and survey her surroundings. She was in her room, the space barely illuminated by a dying fire. Mama and baba slept on cots beside her bed. She shifted to get more comfortable. Her bed creaked and mama sprang up from her cot.

"You are better!" she said.

"Yes, mama" Omolewa managed to say, her voice a low growl.

Mama came to her and hugged her tighter this time before kissing her on her cheeks and forehead.

"If you had died, I would have died too," she whispered.

Mama words made her cry.

"I was in Eda's hands," she said. "She told me what happened. She told me everything."

Mama wiped her tears away.

"Are you sure it was Eda?" she asked. "Someone in your condition is bound to see many things."

"No mama. I am sure," Omolewa replied. "She told me the woman who sold us the fruit was not aware of its danger. She told me I must be diligent and that I should trust no one beyond those who love me most."

"What else did she tell you?" mama asked.

"She told me I have three mothers now," Omolewa said.

Mama smiled. "If Eda watches you, all will be well."

"She did not promise that," Omolewa said. "She told me I must be diligent."

A beam of light pierced the darkness as her bedroom door opened. A guard with a lantern entered, followed by the Bene. Omolewa became nervous as they approached. Her apprehension was not relieved by the worried look on the Bene's face.

"I heard you would be well enough for visitors," the Bene said. "I could not wait until morning. How do you feel?"

"As you can see, she is better," mama answered, her voice quaking with emotion. "You said we would be safe here. We were safer in Nacala."

The Bene looked at mama, clearly annoyed. She turned her attention back to Omolewa.

"Danger would have eventually come for you," the Bene replied. "Be thankful that you were here when it did. Otherwise Omolewa would be dead."

The Bene turned her attention to Omolewa. She shared her mother's misgivings, but she knew what the Bene said was true. If this had happened in Nacala she would not be alive.

"It is a sad day when I cannot protect those I love in my own city," the Bene said. "We've always known there were enemies among us, but we assumed they were too weak to strike. They knew what would happen if they did. Apparently, they must be confident in not being found. We will show them different."

She stood with her guard's help.

"Our priority now is to keep Omolewa safe," she continued. "Kulal made a suggestion which I think is wise. We will send Omolewa to the dry season palace. It is easily defended, with servants that are completely loyal to us."

"The dry season palace?" mama looked skeptical. "Sounds like a better trap."

"I can assure you it is not," the Bene replied. "We normally make a spectacle of our journey, but this will not be the case this time. Only a small group will travel to the palace, and they will leave under the cover of night."

"We will be ready," mama said.

"You will not be going," the Bene replied.

Mama's eyes went wide. "Then neither will Lewa."

"Listen to me," the Bene said. "In order for her to be safe all must appear as normal. If your family leaves, those who seek to harm Omolewa will know she is gone."

"Are you going?" mama asked.

"No. I will stay here as well. She will be accompanied by Kulal, Kashta and a few others. Both men are known to travel frequently."

"They will notice I am gone if no one sees me," Omolewa said.

"Palesa will stand in your stead," Omolewa replied. "She will follow your daily routine until we root out who is threatening your life."

"She will be in danger!" Omolewa said.

The Bene's expression did not change. "She volunteered."

Omolewa knew those words were not true. Palesa was being forced to do so because of their trip to the market.

"I will leave you now," the Bene said. "You will depart for the palace two weeks after the healer says you are well. Until then you will rest."

The Bene came to Omolewa then touched her forehead.

"I am so sorry you have to go through this," she said. "If I could change it all I would. But these are our times. We must rise to the challenge."

She nodded to mother then left the room. Mama's expression turned grim as soon as the door closed.

"I am going with you," she said.

"No mama," Omolewa replied. "The Bene's plan is good."

"Is it? How does she know that no one waits in the dry season palace ready to strike?"

"She doesn't," Omolewa replied. "I'm sure she will have the palace scoured by her guards before we set off on our journey."

"I do not trust her," mama said.

Omolewa remembered Eda's words.

"I do not either, at least not entirely," Omolewa said. "I do think she wants to keep me alive, for what reason I don't know."

"That does not make me feel better," mama said.

"I think she sends me to the palace for good intentions," Omolewa continued. "What I fear is what will happen when I return."

"She may have been the woman who gave birth to you, but she is not your mother. She thinks of you as an object to be played in a game."

Omolewa shoulders slumped.

"I am," she said. "I just don't know what that game is."

She hugged her mama tight.

"But I will find out," she said. "I promise. And I will use whatever strength I have to end it."

* * *

A week passed before Omolewa was strong enough to walk. Palesa joined her during that time, her constant companion throughout the rehabilitation. Few words were spoken between them, the roles each was to play erected an invisible barrier between them. After two weeks Omolewa was able to resume her lessons again, albeit in a much weaker state. Kashta kept the tasks simple, but also began to teach her the subjects that would help her manipulate smaller objects, those that were invisible to the naked eye.

"Kamit scholars believe that the world consists of particles so small they cannot be seen, yet they are the center of all that surrounds us," he said that morning. "We also believe in the intangible spirit that gives them life."

"Ashé," Omolewa said. "It is the spirit of which you speak. Every child knows that. But these particles?"

"They are the foundation of life," Kashta continued. "To be aware of them, to be able to manipulate them through physical means as well as with ashé is the next step to incredible power."

"Do you know any sonchai that can do so?" she asked.

"No," Kashta replied. "There have been only a few, and some of them live today. Unfortunately, most are not our friends."

An ominous weight settled on Omolewa shoulders. "Why are you telling me this?" she asked.

"Because you have the potential to become one of them," Kashta replied.

"I'm not sure I want to be," she said. "It seems the more I know the more my life is in danger."

Kashta approached her, grabbing a chair along the way. He sat beside her then did something unexpected. He took her hand then patted it, like a father would to his worried child.

"I am going to speak to you as an uncle to his favorite niece," he began. "Over these months I have done something I swore I would not do, something I disciplined myself against ever since I took an oath to become a teacher. I've grown fond of you Omolewa."

"It seems that everyone wishes me to be their child," she said.

Kashta laughed. "It does, doesn't it? You are a charming and bright girl. Under different circumstances I could see you being a well-known scholar, possibly running your own academy in Kamit."

"Or maybe Nacala," Omolewa added.

Kashta grinned. "Yes, Nacala. That would be impressive. However, you have been born in times that require a different use of your skills."

"Tell me what's going on," Omolewa said. "I need to know."

"Yes, you do," Kashta replied. "You know of how the Cleave came to be, don't you?"

"Yes," she replied. "Daarila became angry with the people of Ki Khanga because their wars had spilled into the spiritual realm. He decided to rid the world of us once and for all. He forged the Great Axe which he used to destroy our world. As the axe struck, his wife Eda interfered, preventing him from cutting Ki Khanga into pieces. The Cleave is the scar left by his axe, and we are what remained of those who once angered him."

"That is good," Kashta said. "But the story does not end there. There are those that believe Daarila is still not happy with us. They believe he will one day return to finish his work. They have dedicated themselves to making sure it happens."

"Are these the people that threaten me?"

"Yes. They are the people who attacked our dhow, and they are most likely the people behind your poisoning."

"You said most likely," Omolewa said. "Are there other reasons someone in Zimbabwa would want me dead?"

"Yes," Kashta said. "The Bene's lineage has controlled this land for centuries. While most Zimbabwans are content, there are others that wish to see their downfall simply because they wish to take their place."

"Rival families," Omolewa said.

"Exactly. Your story is known among all Zimbabwans. Those who oppose the Bene, however few they are, know how much you mean to her. If they harm you, they weaken the Bene. If the Bene's rule becomes erratic, it justifies them calling for her removal by the elders. However, it will not be so simple."

"Why is that?" Omolewa asked.

"You know why," Kashta replied.

"The Bene masters ashé," Omolewa replied.

Kashta nodded. "And you have only seen a fraction of her strength. She is one of the most powerful sonchai I've ever encountered outside of Kamit. The trait runs strong in her bloodline, although many have not developed it. It runs especially strong among the women. Kulal is powerful, but his power pales in comparison to the Bene. You, on the other hand, have the potential to be as powerful as she, if not more so. Which is your presence causes a complicated situation."

Kashta's explanation gave her the strength to ask the next question.

"Did the Bene kill her husband?" she asked.

Kashta's face turned grim. "Yes."

Fear trickled into Omolewa's mind.

"If she would kill her husband and brothers, then what would she do to me?"

"You underestimate a mother's love for her child," Kashta said. "You and Kulal are her only allies. She loves you just as much as she does him, even though you were raised by others. Her brothers were petty men who meant to see her dead; that is how power can twist the mind. Her husband had his own ambitions for the stool. I believe he would have lived it he had not deceived her in believing he truly loved her."

Omolewa thought on all that Kashta said.

"So, the Bene loves me and wishes to control me," Omolewa concluded. "What happens if she realizes she cannot? What if she begins to suspect that I might challenge her?"

"That is why it is so important that you learn as much as possible as soon as you can," Kashta said. "I don't believe you will challenge her. I know you want no part of any of this. But a war is coming that you must take part. I just hope that war is not between the two of you."

Kulal entered the room, his face more serious than Omolewa had ever witnessed.

"I'm sorry to interrupt your scheming," he said. "But I must steal a few moments of my sister's time. We will be traveling soon, and she has yet to become familiar with her quaggat."

Omolewa moaned.

"Must I? I was hoping I could ride in a wagon."

"Our departure is to seem normal," Kulal said. "If you come rolling out of the palace in a wagon and guards flanking you it will be anything but. When we depart it will be you and I. Kashta will follow later. And we will be riding quaggats."

"We will have plenty of time for training once we reach the Dry Season Palace," Kashta said.

Omolewa trudged behind Kulal to the stables. She was not looking forward to this training. The first time she tried to ride one of the volatile beasts she was thrown and almost kicked in the head. The second time was not much different. Now she would be expected to ride one for miles. This would not be good. Not good at all.

"Remember what I told you the last time," Kulal said. "You have to establish your control as soon as you approach your mount. Direct eye contact, forceful approach."

"I tried that," she replied. "It didn't work, twice."

"The quaggat didn't believe you," Kulal said.

"Maybe I should hit it with a stick," Omolewa said.

"Hit a quaggat once and it will become your enemy forever," Kulal said. "Your quaggat is your servant. You must establish your dominance over it. If you do, it will do anything you ask. It will even die for you."

"You're exaggerating," Omolewa said.

Kulal stopped then turned to her. "No, I'm not."

There was a story behind that gaze, but Omolewa was in no mood to listen to it, so she didn't ask. She also had a feeling that Kulal was in no mood to tell it.

When they entered the stables two quaggats had been saddled. The large black and gold stallion Omolewa recognized as Kulal's; the brown and tan quaggat was unknown to her.

"This is not my quaggat," she said.

"It's not," Kulal replied. "Sometimes a person and a quaggat just don't mesh. For those without means it's a situation one must live with, but since you are the Bene's daughter you have a choice. The stable master thought this one might be more amenable to you."

"You mean I have to start over?" Omolewa whined.

"Yes, you do."

Omolewa took a deep breath then focused on the quaggat's large black eyes. The animal stared back unmoved. She strode directly to it then took its head between her hands. She tried Kulal's way, and it didn't work. It was time to try something different.

"I wouldn't do that if . . ."

"Be quiet, Kulal," Omolewa said. "We're having a conversation."

Omolewa continued to stare into the beast's eyes. She remembered the day she acquired Pik-Pik. As she looked into the ferret's eyes something happened, something that bonded them to this day. She knew now it was her hidden abilities. If it happened once, it could happen again.

She reached into the quaggat's mind. The beast jerked then hissed.

"Be careful!" Kulal shouted.

Omolewa did not move. This would be a deeper connection she realized, one much stronger than the bond she shared with Pik-Pik. She lost herself in the quaggat's mind; she ran with others like it across grass fields, reveling in the feeling of unbridled freedom. Images flashed in rapid succession, feeding, flight, mating, living and dying. She realized that she was not experiencing the life of the single quaggat but the experiences of an entire herd. She had gone too deep. She pulled back and the quaggat calmed. This beast's life was much simpler, a birth in a sheltered barn and bonding with a much smaller herd. The pain of separation from its mother and the solitary life that caused it and other quaggats to have such a difficult disposition.

"You must stop separating them," Omolewa said absently. "That's why they are so mean."

Kulal looked puzzled. "What?"

Omolewa didn't hear him. She was back into the mind of her quaggat. Yes, she was her quaggat now, not as an owner, but as a companion. She pulled her head away from the quaggat then stroked her neck. The quaggat licked her hand with its rough tongue and Omolewa smiled.

"We understand each other, don't we?" she said.

The quaggat quivered in response.

"I don't believe this," Kulal said. "I've never seen a quaggat lick its master."

"I'm not her master," Omolewa said. "We're friends."

Omolewa slowly worked her way to the saddle then climbed into it. She leaned onto the quaggat's neck then whispered into its ears. The words were more for her than for the beast.

"Do I have your permission?" she asked.

The beast neighed.

"Thank you," she replied.

When she looked up Kulal stared at her with incredulous eyes.

"By the ancestors," he said.

"Shall we ride?" Omolewa asked.

They rode throughout the courtyard to get Omolewa used to the saddle then set out from the palace into the streets.

The press of people made her quaggat nervous, so Omolewa patted her neck and whispered to her during the trek.

"She doesn't like the crowds," Omolewa said to Kulal. "Can we ride outside the city?"

"Follow me," Kulal said.

They followed the wide avenue that led to the southern portion of the city. Omolewa's quaggat relaxed as the crowds thinned. As the road narrowed and the buildings gave way to the forest Omolewa's quaggat felt joy.

"This is more like it," she said. "I think my…"

The quaggat burst into a full gallop, running headlong down the trail.

"Whoa!" Omolewa shouted. The quaggat did not heed her words; she was free and taking full advantage of it. Omolewa could do nothing but hold on tight, yet she wasn't afraid. As fast as the quaggat ran she was still holding back, making sure she did not lose Omolewa as she enjoyed the openness of the forest. She finally slowed then trotted to a patch of green grass. She lowered her head then munched on the vegetation.

Kulal caught up with them a few moments later. He guided his quaggat next to Omolewa's and it began to eat as well.

"You have a racer on your hands," he said. "I've never seen a quaggat run so fast so far, especially with a rider on its back."

"She loves the forest," Omolewa said. "I think we will be fine on the trail to the palace tomorrow."

"So, your ashé lets you communicate with her?" he asked.

"Yes," Omolewa replied. "It's the same with Pik-Pik, but this bond is deeper."

"Amazing," Kulal said. "You must give her a name."

"I don't think so," Omolewa said. "We know each other."

"It's only proper. The rest of us need to know what to call her."

Omolewa patted the quaggat's neck. "Do you want a name?"

The quaggat shuddered as it continued to eat.

"She doesn't care," Omolewa replied. "I will give you a Kiswala name. I will call you Furaha."

The quaggat neighed and Omolewa grinned.

"We have agreed," she said.

"Excellent," Kulal said. "We need to get back to the palace. It will be dark soon."

He reined his quaggat about then headed back toward the trail. Furaha snorted.

"I know," Omolewa said. "It's the way he was taught and the way his quaggat learned. We will teach them a better way, okay?"

Furaha neighed then trotted to the trail. They caught up with Kulal then fell in step. Kulal glanced at her, a concerned look on his face.

"Furaha will be good during our journey, but what about you?" he asked. "It will be your first time away from your family."

Omolewa tried not to think about it, but now Kulal had laid it out before her. Her stomach churned in response.

"I don't know," she answered. "I know this is necessary, but I wish there was another way. I must go, though. Not because the Bene wants it, but because I don't want to put my family in danger."

"Our mama," he said.

"What?"

"You keep calling her the Bene," he replied. "She is our mama. You can call her that when you and I are alone."

"I can't," Omolewa said. "I know who she is, but I still don't see her that way. I did not grow up with her as you did."

"She is a generous and loving woman when given the chance," Kulal said.

"That is hard for me to believe," Omolewa replied.

"You must understand her circumstances. She grew up in a world where she had to compete with her brothers for her place. Whatever she did, she did so because she had to."

Omolewa hesitated before revealing what she had learned. She looked away from Kulal and concentrated on the road ahead.

"What is it you wish to ask?" he said.

"Nothing," Omolewa replied.

"Go ahead and ask me," he said. "We can't have anything between us."

Omolewa swallowed hard before facing her brother again.

"What about our baba?"

Kulal stiffened and a look of uncertainty distorted his otherwise handsome face.

"I cannot speak on that," he finally said.

"Why?" Omolewa asked. "Don't you want to know how he died, and why she killed him?"

"She had no choice!" he shouted. His anger quickly subsided to sadness.

"She had no choice."

"Do you know this for sure or is this what you were told…by her."

"What are you trying to say, Lewa?" he asked, the anger rising again in his voice.

Omolewa contemplated whether she should tell him exactly how she felt. She did not need Kulal as an enemy, not with other mysterious people trying to take her life.

"I am sure she was justified," she said despite believing otherwise. "It seems the title of Bene is more important to some people than their own family."

Omolewa regretted her last words, but it was too late to take them back. Kulal looked at her confused.

"I know she loves me and would never harm me," he said. "And I have no ambitions beyond what I am and who I am right now. If the time comes that I am chosen to be Bene, it will be because mama has been called home to take her place with the ancestors. There will be no threat to her rule from me, nor should there be from you."

"I'm glad you are so sure," she said.

"And you're not?" Kulal asked.

"Why should I be?"

"Because ever since you been gone all she has done is worry about you." She could hear the emotion in his voice.

"I don't think I turned out to be what she imagined me to be," Omolewa said. "Our relationship will never be as close as yours is to her. I think in time she will realize that the child that has been with her all his life is the child she should cherish the most."

"Thank you for saying that," Kulal said. "You show wisdom at such a young age. Unfortunately, we both have an influence on how she feels."

"I think she will learn in time. It takes adults longer because they think they already know everything, especially if they are a Bene."

Kulal laughed and Omolewa did as well. They rode back to the palace talking of silly and unimportant things, both done with serious topics. Furaha was clearly disturbed as she led her back into her stall, snorting and stomping her hooves. Omolewa knelt before her and took her head into her hands again.

"I'll be back," she whispered. "Tomorrow we will go on a very long ride, and I will make sure that once we arrive at our destination you won't have to live in one of these things."

The quaggat calmed then licked her face.

Omolewa went directly to her parents' chamber. Her siblings rushed her with their usual exuberance, followed by Pik-Pik who climbed her then wrapped her thin body around her shoulders. Mama and baba smile as she approached, but she could see the worry and concern in their gestures. Mama hugged her tight, as did baba.

"How was your ride?" mama asked.

"It was good," she replied. "The Bene gave me another quaggat. This one was much better." She decided not to tell them how she bonded with the animal; they were nervous enough about her growing abilities.

"I want a quaggy!" Kazija announced.

"Me, too!" Diwani chimed.

"I guess you'll get one one day," Omolewa said. Mama glared at her.

"Or maybe not."

"Come eat and get some rest," mama said. "You have a long trip ahead."

She ate heartily, not realizing how much the day had taxed her. That night she played with Diwani and Kazija, her patience with their antics much higher than usual. Mama and baba watched, occasionally exchanging words too low for her to understand. They were up to something; she was sure it involved her. She would find out in due time.

mama and baba approached her after she put her siblings to bed.

"You don't have to go if you don't want to," baba said.

"I have no choice," she replied. "The Bene has decreed it."

Mama and baba looked at each other.

"We can leave tonight," mama said.

"What?" Omolewa was stunned.

"How?"

"I arranged for a dhow to take us away," baba said. They are waiting for us."

For a brief moment Omolewa felt a burden lift from her. If they left, she wouldn't have to deal with the unknown looming before her. Maybe these enemies of the Bene would stop trying to kill her if they knew she had no intentions of fighting them. But then Kashta's words came to mind and she frowned.

"No," she said. "We can't leave. I must do this."

"This is not your decision," baba said. "We are your parents. If we decide to do this, you must obey."

"That is true, baba," she replied. "If you insist, we will leave tonight. I will pack my things and go with you. But do you really think the Bene will let us walk out of the palace and return to Nacala?"

Baba looked away.

"If I can't protect my daughter, what good am I?" he said.

Omolewa went to her baba then hugged him.

"You have protected me," she said. "You took me away from here when it was not safe and you raised me as your own, you and mama both. But now I must do what I was raised to do. When I am done then we can speak of other things."

Mama smiled. "Look who talks with reason. It seems you are more prepared to accept your responsibility than we are."

Omolewa hugged mama.

"I'm not ready for any of this," she said. "I don't know what else to do. I just want us to be happy."

"We want the same thing," baba said. "It seems our fate has been written; all we can do is follow it and hope for the best."

"We should get some sleep," mama said. "Tomorrow is a big day for us."

"I don't want to sleep," Omolewa said.

"Staying awake all night won't stop the sun from rising," Baba said. "The day will arrive whether we like it or not."

They slept together once again in the large bed. Omolewa did not think she could sleep but she did, the day taxing her more than she realized. She was the first to wake. She lifted her head slightly to gaze at her slumbering family, wondering if this was the last time she would see them this way. The Bene, Kashta and Kulal all insisted she would be safe at the Dry Season Palace, but she still could not grasp their confidence. Before she left Nacala no one had ever threatened her life until that fateful day the black dhow arrived in the harbor. Ever since then her life had been on edge. She watched them a moment longer before leaving the bed to dress. Mama was the first to awake.

"So, it is time," she said.

Omolewa looked at mama with tears in her eyes.

"Let me help you," mama said.

Omolewa didn't need mama's assistance, but she did not refuse. She dressed, with mama picking out what she should wear. By the time she was done the others had awakened. Baba sat watching them, his morose face causing

Omolewa more grief. She knew what he wanted to do, but she also knew it wouldn't work. There was only one path they could walk and prepared or not, she would take it.

The family arrived at breakfast in silence. The Bene, Kashta and Kulal waited, their mood subdued. The servants moved about efficiently as always. Omolewa had no appetite but forced herself to eat. She did not know how long they would be on the road before she had the opportunity to eat again.

The Bene finally broke the silence.

"Kulal, is everything set?" she asked.

"Yes, mama" he said, losing his usual decorum. "The servants departed a week ago. The Palace should be aired out and clean by the time we arrive. Omolewa and I will leave after breakfast with a small contingent. The goal is to appear as a hunting trip. Kashta will come two days later. He will head south as if leaving for the coast then divert north once he is far enough away for his changes not to be seen."

"I will travel alone," Kashta said.

"Is that wise?" the Bene asked.

"Not wise, but necessary. If there is someone or something threatening us, I hope to draw it out. I would be a better target than Kulal and Omolewa would be together."

"You shouldn't be by yourself," Omolewa said.

Kashta smiled. "I can handle myself. And if not, my replacement will be more than capable of continuing your training."

They finished the morning meal then parted ways. There were no special words from the Bene, just a heartfelt look and a touch on Omolewa's shoulder. Her family followed her and Kulal to the stables where the others waited. There were two guards and two donkeys loaded with provisions. A stablehand held the reins of Kulal's quaggat. Omolewa smiled when she saw Furaha being led from the stables by Palesa. The woman walked up to her with a smile on her face then handed her the reins.

"Thank you," Omolewa said before hugging her friend. "I'm sorry you've been drawn into this. I've been nothing but bad luck to you."

"You have been my friend," Palesa replied. "I am thankful for it. The Bene asked me to do this duty and I accepted."

Omolewa climbed into the saddle.

"I will make it up to you. I promise," she said to Palesa.

"Be safe and come back," Palesa said. "That is all I ask."

Palesa grinned then walked away. Omolewa watched her, realizing that she was one of the few friends she had.

Furaha snorted, drawing her attention. She patted the quaggat's neck.

"Be patient. We're leaving soon."

Pik-Pik scurried around her neck then fussed in her ear.

"Don't be jealous," Omolewa said. "Furaha is a new friend. You'll come to like her."

Furaha raised her head then snorted as she looked at the agitated ferret.

"I see you're not the only one unhappy about this," Omolewa said. "You two will just have to work it out."

Pik-Pik nipped at her ear.

"Ow! One more time and you're staying here!"

Pik-Pik settled against her neck, but not before hissing at Furaha.

Kulal rode up beside her, his bright smile easing her mood.

"Are you ready?" he asked.

"No."

"Neither am I," he said with a smile.

Her family gathered around her. Mama gave her a loaf of bread wrapped in cloth.

"Don't eat it all at one time," she said.

"I won't." Omolewa took the bread then stuffed it in her saddle bag.

Baba came to her then handed her his wrist knife.

"It's probably too big for your forearm," he said. "Wear it on your arm."

Omolewa leaned toward baba, and he strapped the knife to her bicep then kissed her cheek.

Omolewa looked at Diwani and Kazija.

"You two behave while I'm gone," she said.

"We won't," Diwani said.

"We won't," Kazija repeated.

"Then no sweets for you when I come back," Omolewa said. "I'll eat it all myself."

"We'll be good!" Diwani shouted.

Omolewa smiled. "I thought so."

"We must go," Kulal said. "We're losing daylight."

The small band rode to the palace gate, her family walking beside them on foot. As they advanced through the gate her family waved, mama and baba with tears in their eyes as Diwani and Kazija jumped up and down waving. Omolewa reached up to brush away the tears rolling down her cheeks. She took one more look then turned way. She was striking out on her own for the first time in her life.

"Eda protect me," she whispered.

- 9 -

The forest mist appeared as they reached the foothills and continued to blanket them throughout the day. Until that point their journey had been blessed by a string of sunny yet cool days, the temperature moderating the closer they came to the mountains. Omolewa pulled the rain cloak about her tighter; Pik-Pik rode her shoulders under the protective garment. The pleasant days helped ease her mind, but the gloom of the mist depressed her, and she thought of her family. Furaha seemed to sense her mood and shook her head as she snorted. Omolewa patted her neck.

"I know," she said. "I haven't been much company lately. I think I'll feel better once we reach the Palace."

Kulal appeared on her right.

"Are you talking to that quaggat again?" he asked.

"Yes," Omolewa replied. "You should talk to yours, too."

Kulal laughed. "Really? And what does one say to a quaggat?"

"Anything, as long as it's nice. It's not the words, it's the feelings. They are nice as long as you respect them."

"Sounds like something to try later," Kulal said. Furaha nipped at Kulal's leg.

"Hey!" he shouted.

Omolewa grinned. "See. I told you."

Kulal rolled his eyes. "We're near the palace. If the servants have done their job, there will be a warm fire waiting for us."

"I hope so," Omolewa replied.

"How are you?" Kulal asked.

"I'm okay. I miss my family."

"That's understandable. Once you resume your training you won't have time to miss them. Kashta can be a real task master. Here your total focus will be honing your gift, and from what I've seen Kashta will keep you quite busy."

"And what will you do?" Omolewa asked.

"Assist when I can," he said. "And make sure we are secure."

Omolewa didn't like how that sounded.

"I thought the reason we came here was that no one would bother us."

"That's true, but you can never be too sure," Kulal answered. "These are dangerous times. Loyalties have been compromised. We must keep vigilant."

The Dry Season Palace emerged slowly from the haze and vegetation, a man-made mountain of black granite. Its appearance stunned Omolewa; she expected a smaller, more intimate building, but the Dry Season Palace was every bit as imposing as the main palace. Unlike the central stronghold, a recently cleared road separated the palace from the surrounding foliage. Kulal took a small whistle from his shirt then blew two sharp notes which were quickly answered. Moments later two guards rode up to them on large quaggats, welcoming smiles on their face.

"Welcome, *nevanji*," the lead rider said.

"Greetings, Takunda," Kulal replied. "Is the palace ready?"

"As ready as can be expected," he answered. "It had become the residence of a very difficult troop of monkeys. We've run them off . . . for now."

"Looks like we may have more company than expected," Kulal said.

"It is not humorous to me, nevanji," Takunda said. "I hate monkeys."

Kulal gestured to Omolewa.

"Takunda, this is my sister Omolewa."

Takunda's eyes widened. "Your sister?"

He and the other warrior dismounted then prostrated before Omolewa.

"Please forgive me, *mamoyo*," he said to Omolewa. "I was not aware Nevanji Kulal had a sister, let alone was bringing you with him."

"I told you we kept things as secret as possible," Kulal whispered to Omolewa.

"It's nice to meet you, Takunda," Omolewa said. "What is your companion's name?"

The man looked up, a smile on his face.

"I am Simbarashe," he said. "It is an honor to meet you."

"Enough formalities," Kulal said. "Let's get inside. It's been a long journey."

They followed the guards to the palace entrance, a large metàl gate tarnished by exposure. The courtyard of the palace was a surprise; instead of the wide area of packed dirt the Dry Season palace courtyard was a garden. Flowering shrubs bordered the interior paver brick path which eventually expanded into an open area bordered by fruit trees.

"It is no wonder the monkeys come inside," Omolewa said. "This is a forest feast."

"Mama loves this garden," Kulal said. "It allows her to enjoy the bush without having to actually enter it."

"I take it our mama is not fond of the forest."

"No, she's not," Kulal said. "Mosquitoes and biting flies are fond of her, however."

The palace buzzed with workers. Some swept the ramparts while others pruned the flora. Stable workers waited for them in the courtyard center; Kulal dismounted his quaggat then handed the reins to one of them. Omolewa waved her stable hand away.

"It is her first time here," she said to the young woman. "Mine, too. She would prefer I do this. What is your name?"

The woman looked at her, clearly surprised.

"My name, mamoyo?"

"Omolewa smiled. "Yes, your name."

"Anenyasha."

Where do you want her?"

Anenyasha looked at Kulal, clearly confused.

"She talks to her quaggat," he said as he shrugged. "They're friends."

"This way, mamoyo," the woman said.

Omolewa followed the worker to the stables. They were walking down the stalls when Furaha stopped then nudged her hand.

"This one?" Omolewa asked.

Furaha bumped her hand again.

"This one," Omolewa told Anenyasha. She let Furaha's reins go, and she walked into the stall, turned about then lay down. To Omolewa's surprise Pik-Pik jumped from her shoulders then joined Furaha, nestling in the straw at her side.

"So, when did you two become friends?" Omolewa said.

"Don't worry about them," Anenyasha said. "We will take good care of them."

"If you don't, they'll tell me," Omolewa replied.

Anenyasha looked skeptical. "Yes, mamoyo."

Omolewa laughed as she ambled up to Kulal. It was good her pets were friends; she would worry less about them.

"Come, let me show you the palace," Kulal said. "It's not as grand as home but it's very comfortable. Since there is no one else here you get to pick your room. Unless the monkeys beat you to it."

"I'll deal with the monkeys," Omolewa said.

"What? You'll have a conversation with them, too?"

Omolewa grinned. "If I have to."

Kulal rolled his eyes. "Follow me."

They entered the palace through the servant's entrance into the kitchen. The room bustled with cooks and other workers preparing the palace for its meager occupants. A few stole glances at Omolewa and she smiled in return. They emerged into one of the corridors.

"This hall leads to the grand meeting room," Kulal said. "We'll pass through it on our way to the family chambers."

"Our mother holds assembly here? I thought this was a retreat."

"No rest for the Bene," Kulal replied. "Her duties are less formal here, but they never end. Visitors are constantly arriving from the city, and the local chiefs take advantage of her being so close. They come with their praises, criticisms, and disputes. It can be a busy place but not nearly as active as the Central palace. For us it will be very quiet."

The assembly room was less elaborate than its Central Palace counterpart. A few soapstone sculptures occupied the corners of the room and there were several wooden benches near the empty dais where the Bene dispensed her judgment and wisdom. As Kulal said, there was not much to see.

The hallway leading to the family rooms was more intimate. Its narrow confines opened into another large room, a circular space with a fireplace in the center. A small fire burned, the smoke rising to an opening in the high ceiling. Doorways punctuated the diameter, each with a distinct and attractive archway. The Bene's archway was the largest and most elaborate, the black stone accented with gold and jewels.

"I'll take that room," Omolewa announced.

"It's yours," Kulal said.

Omolewa's eyes went wide. "Really?"

"Why not? No one here but us. However, it would be interesting if mama decided to show up."

"I'll choose another room," she said.

"Actually, the rooms on either side of hers are ours."

"Why would there be a room for me?"

"She knew that one day you would come home," Kulal said. "It's her gift. It was also in her power to make her prediction come true just in case you didn't."

"I think I will stay in her room," Omolewa said.

Kulal prostrated before her.

"Welcome to the Dry Season Palace, my Bene!" he announced.

Omolewa laughed as Kulal jumped to his feet then marched to the room. Omolewa following with a regal gait. He grasped the door handle then bowed as he opened the door and stepped aside. Omolewa nodded her head as she passed him. When she entered the room, she her face dropped. It was empty. Kulal burst out laughing.

"Where is everything?" Omolewa asked.

Kulal laughed for a few more moments before answering.

"All the rooms are empty," he said. "We bring what we need from the Central Palace. The procession here is quite a sight."

Omolewa cuffed his shoulder and he laughed again.

"Don't worry," he said. "We have the necessities. Do you still want this room?"

"Yes," Omolewa said.

"Good. I'll have the servants prepare it. Come, let's go to the training room."

They passed through the assembly room again then took a different corridor to a smaller area. There was one door on the opposite side of the space. It opened into the training room. The room was very similar to the training room in the Central Palace despite being significantly smaller.

"This is where you will spend most of your time," Kulal said. "Kashta will continue building your ashé while I'll be in charge of the rest of your training."

"What will you teach me?" Omolewa asked.

Kulal took out his sword. "I will teach you to fight."

"Will that be necessary?" she asked. "It seems to me if I can master my ashé I won't need weapons."

"And what happens when you confront someone whose ashé is equal to yours? Besides, it's more than just weapons skills," Kulal said. "It's about discipline and tactics."

Omolewa felt weakness in her legs. She located a nearby stool then sat. Kulal took a seat beside her.

"Are you okay?" Kulal asked.

"All this talk about fighting," she said. "I know I helped you and Kashta on the dhow, and I understand what I must do. But I am not a fighter, Kulal. Baba is, but not me."

"Sometimes we don't have a choice," Kulal replied. "I pray to Eda that you never have to use your skills in such a way, but the times dictate that you will. So, you must be prepared, and you must put all your effort is being the best you can be. This is a road you were destined to travel."

"Destined?" Omolewa folded her arms against a chill inside her far worse than that of the room. "You say that as if I was born to do this."

"You were, in a way," Kulal said.

"So, the Bene conceived me for this responsibility?"

"You are a child of lineage," Kulal said. "You are also a child blessed with ashé. With both comes great duty."

"If only I could choose how I lived," she said.

"No one can," Kulal said. "Even the freest is confined to conform. The world is a web and we're all trapped."

Omolewa looked at her brother and noticed the sadness in his face.

"You feel it, too," she said.

"Yes. But there is nothing I can do about it. It seems odd complaining about privilege. Many are those who wished they had our problems. Those desires vanish when you are sitting on a quaggat watching your enemy charge at you, intent on your demise. Digging a furrow with a rusted hoe doesn't seem so bad then."

Kulal stood suddenly. "Enough brooding. I'm hungry."

Omolewa stood beside him. "Me, too."

"Let's see what the servants have cooked up. If I have to eat another piece of smoked beef I'm falling on my sword."

Omolewa followed her brother back into the courtyard garden. Cooking fires had been built on the stone sections with large pots hanging over them. The smell of goat caused Omolewa mouth to water.

"I didn't realize I was so hungry," she said.

"Neither did I," Kulal replied. "Do you think it would burn much if I stuck my hand into the pot?"

Omolewa laughed. "I'm sure it would."

Their wait for a meal was not long; the servants placed sitting mats around the fires and everyone was served large bowls of stew and bread. Servants and lineage ate together, unlike the main palace.

"I like this," Omolewa said. "I've never felt comfortable eating with the Bene and the others. It's so formal."

"Enjoy it while you can," Kulal said. "Mama would become a storm if she saw us. She is very strict when it comes to decorum. But it is her life. It's the only way she knows to live."

"You were raised in her life as well, yet you sit among those who serve you with ease. I can tell they love you. You would make a great Bene, for all your people would see you as their own."

"I'm glad you think so," Kulal said. "If only mama thought the same."

Kulal lifted his bowl, drinking the remaining stew. He wiped his mouth then let out a loud burp which caused laughter. Omolewa and the others did the same, trying to outdo Kulal with the volume of their burps.

The servants cleared the mats as the sun set below the hills. One of the servants handed Omolewa a lit torch and they made their way inside the palace. She walked with Kulal back to the rooms.

"Get your rest," he said. "Tomorrow will be the beginning of a busy time for you."

"I will," she replied. "Thank you, Kulal."

Her brother looked puzzled. "For what?"

"For being a true brother," she said. "I have always been the eldest and the responsibility has sometimes been great. It's good to have someone else to shoulder the burden."

"You're my sister," he said. "And not just by blood. I felt this way the first time I saw you."

He kissed her on the forehead and Omolewa giggled.

"Now go to sleep and dream of pleasant things."

Kulal entered his room then closed his door. Omolewa looked at the ornate door leading into the Bene's room then laughed. She was foolish to take this room. She pushed open the door, walking in with the torch before her to light the way. The servants had set up the Bene's bed with a nightstand beside it. A large bowl filled with fruit and a drinking gourd rested on the nightstand. On the bed were night clothes which Omolewa changed into quickly. She ate one fruit then took a sip of water before climbing into the bed. The comfortable mattress and soft head rest were an exquisite contrast to sleeping on the road for so long. She fell to sleep quickly, hoping to dream of pleasant things.

- 1 0 -

Omolewa's training began early as Kulal promised. Her physical teaching consisted of hand-to-hand combat and weapons, all supervised by Kulal. He may have been a sweet and attentive brother during their journey, but in the training room he was hard and relentless. Baba taught her a few techniques to defend herself, but never was his training this thorough. Kulal would show her a move and then make her practice it over and over again. On this particular day she practiced a simple front kick until her leg was numb. Her last kick was so weak she stumbled into Kulal after she brought it to the floor. He caught her as he laughed.

"I guess it's time for a break," he said.

"That time came thirty minutes ago," she replied.

Kulal strolled to the bench against the wall as Omolewa hobbled behind him favoring her right leg.

"Why must I do this so many times?" she said.

"Muscle memory," Kulal replied. "Do you think when you pick up a fork or a spoon?"

"No," Omolewa said.

"There was a time when doing such a thing was a difficult task for you," he said. "But you did it every day because you had to. Now you eat without thinking, grabbing your utensil and going about your work."

Omolewa eye brightened. "So, we practice the kick over and over again so I can eat with my foot?"

They laughed and Kulal shoved her shoulder.

"That's exactly it," he said. "I'm teaching you to eat with your foot. Seriously, many believe combat should be complex, that a warrior should know hundreds of techniques in order to defeat their opponent. But real fighting is just the opposite. When you are in a battle, it's best to be quick and decisive. Any hesitation can cost you your life. So, it is better to know only a few techniques but to know them as if they are a part of you. They become instinctive; you see the opening instantly and apply the technique. It can be the difference between life and death."

As Omolewa listened to Kulal she could tell he spoke from experience.

"What is it like to fight in a battle, Kulal?" she asked.

"It is the worst thing ever," he replied. "I hope you never have to go through it. But in case you do, I would rather you be prepared."

"I would too. Will we train with weapons?"

"Yes, but not now. You won't always have your weapons with you, but you'll always have these."

He held up his hands one at a time then his feet.

They drank more coconut water then Kulal stood.

"Are you ready for more front kicks?" he asked.

Omolewa jumped to her feet then tested her leg.

"Ready!" she announced.

Omolewa and Kulal practiced the entire day, interrupted only by servants bringing them food and drink. As the sun descended under the undulating horizon Omolewa was exhausted. She trudged to her room where a bath awaited. As she disrobed, she could smell the aroma of medicinal herbs rising from the warm water. She eased into the liquid and succumbed to its relief, closing her eyes and thinking of home and her family. She wondered how baba and mama were occupying themselves and if Diwani and Kazija were behaving. Her mind eventually drifted to the Bene. Although she wished Omolewa to accept her as her mother, she did much to keep distance between them. Was it because one day they would be rivals? If that was her reason it was ill-founded. Omolewa had no designs on the stool. She was still uncertain she wanted to do what she was being trained to do, let alone rule a country. Kulal was more than capable of governing Zimbabwa; he was smart, well-liked and seemed eager to accept the stool if offered to him.

She shook her head to dispel those thoughts. She needed to relax her mind and body for the coming day. Kulal would no doubt work her to exhaustion, and there was no telling what Kashta had in store for her when he arrived. She finished her bath, readied herself for bed then drifted into a dreamless sleep.

She awoke to tapping on her door. As she sat up the soreness made itself known and she groaned in response. The tapping became an urgent knock.

"I'm coming!" she shouted. She did an awkward shuffle to the door then opened it. Kulal stood before her, a gleaming smile on his face.

"Good morning!" he chimed. "How do you feel?"

"Like I've been beaten with a very large stick for a very long time."

"Excellent!" Kulal replied. "Today I will use an even bigger stick."

"That's not funny," Omolewa said.

"It wasn't intended to be. I'll be waiting in the courtyard."

Omolewa changed from her sleeping garments into her training clothes. As she moved the soreness dissipated; by the time she reached the courtyard she walked normally with the exception of a slight limp. Kulal observed her as she reached the table then sat.

"No kicking today," he said. "We'll work on hand techniques and give your leg some time to heal."

"Thank you," Omolewa said.

She ate the bowl of fruit quickly then drank her fill of water.

"The sonchai comes!"

Omolewa and Kulal looked toward the gate. The servants opened the portal and Kashta rode into the courtyard on a large quaggat, followed by a pair of donkeys loaded with baggage. He dismounted and the servants took his animals to the stables as he strode to the table.

"Greetings, young ones!" he said. His voice was full of energy and excitement. "I assume all has gone well?"

"Welcome, Kashta," Kulal said. "Yes, everything has gone well. I've concentrated on physical training until your arrival."

"Very good," Kashta said as he sat at the table. He looked at Omolewa and smiled.

"Physical discipline is just as important as mental dexterity," he said to her.

"Greetings, Kashta," Omolewa said. "Kulal has been a good teacher."

Kashta cut a playful glance at Kulal. "We will see."

A servant brought a bowl of fruit to the sonchai and he indulged.

"There will be a change in your schedule," he said. "The first portion of your day will be dedicated to your studies, the second portion on physical training. Once I am confident you are progressing well, we will make forays into the forest to work on your herbal training.

"Herbal training?" Omolewa was puzzled. "Am I to be a healer as well?"

"In a way," Kashta said. "There will be times that you will be alone and need healing. If you can do it yourself it will be a benefit. There are also certain floras that can enhance your ability as you learned at the Central palace. These plants differ based on the region."

"There is so much to learn," Omolewa commented.

"And not much time to do so," Kashta said.

"You keep saying that," Omolewa said. "What exactly is about to happen?"

"We will discuss it…eventually," Kashta said. "For now, I need to know where I can set up my things."

"There is a library near the bedrooms," Kulal said. "It's small, but it is all we have."

"It will suffice," Kashta said.

"I will assign servants to help you," Kulal offered.

"I need only someone to show me the way. The rest I can do myself."

Kulal leaned toward Omolewa. "He hates people touching his things."

"I do," Kashta said. "Which is why I don't understand why you keep trying."

"What can I say? I can be annoying sometimes."

Kashta eyes narrowed. "Yes, you can."

Kulal laughed. It seemed to Omolewa that his mood was never foul, yet she had to remember what he did to the men in her home long ago and how he fought the shumba on the road to Zimbabwa. Her brother was kind, playful and generous; but he could also be dangerous.

A servant appeared beside Kashta then bowed.

"May I assist you, sonchai?" she said.

"Take me to the library please," Kashta answered.

The woman extended her hand toward the palace.

"This way, honored guest."

She strolled away and Kashta followed.

"A half a day only," he called out. "I expect to see you in the library at noon."

"I'll be there," Omolewa replied.

She finished her bread then drank her water.

"I'd like to go to the stables before we begin," she said.

Kulal looked puzzled. "Why?"

"To see my friends."

"Your pets are being well taken care of," he said. "Our servants are quite attentive."

"That's good, but they are my friends. I'm sure they miss me."

"How can a …"

Omolewa folded her arms then frowned at her brother.

"Okay, but only for a few minutes," he said. "We have much to do and less time to do it now that Kashta is here."

Omolewa left the table then hurried to the stables. Anenyasha was sweeping out the building; she saw Omolewa and began to prostrate.

"Please don't!" Omolewa said. "You'll get filthy."

"As you wish, mamoyo," she replied.

"Call me Omolewa. We'll save the formalities when Kulal is present."

Anenyasha smiled. "Thank you . . . Omolewa."

"How are my friends?"

"They are doing well. They miss you."

Omolewa was about to ask Anenyasha how she knew when she heard a familiar snort.

"I'm here, Furaha!" she called out.

She found her quaggat standing and shaking her head. Omolewa opened the stall and entered; Furaha backed away.

"You are upset with me," Omolewa said.

Furaha kicked her hind legs. Omolewa approached her slowly then hugged her neck. She felt the quaggat relax then held her tighter.

"I know, but I'm very busy," she said. "I will come back today and we'll go riding. I promise."

Omolewa looked about. "Where is Pik-Pik?"

She was answered by a sharp chirp from above. Pik-Pik scampered across a support beam then clambered down the wall to the stall. She jumped onto Omolewa's shoulder then nipped her ear.

"Ow! I see you are unhappy with me, too. I promise to come back this evening."

"That one has been very mischievous," Anenyasha said. "She won't come for her meals. She prefers the local rodents."

"Thank you for taking care of them."

"It's my pleasure. I will leave you alone with them. I have duties to attend to."

Pik-Pik curled around her neck as Furaha settled into the hay. Omolewa sat down then leaned against her, closing her eyes and clearing her mind. For a few moments she felt complete peace.

"Are you done?" Kulal said.

Omolewa took Pik-Pik from her neck then placed her in the hay. She patted Furaha's neck then stood.

"I'll be back," she said.

She followed Kulal from the stable.

"So how are your friends?" he asked, a smirk on his face.

"They were offended," she replied. "Can we go for a ride later today?"

"Yes, I suppose we can. You should become familiar with the surrounding forest. We'll take Kashta with us. He can begin your herb training."

"Thank you," she said.

The morning combat training was shorter but more intense. By the time they ended Omolewa's clothes were soaked with sweat, as was Kulal's. The servants brought her a change of garments and she hurried to her room to change before meeting Kashta in the library. When she entered, she noticed a new addition to the room; a board mounted on a wooden stand.

"You're on time," he said. "Excellent. Kulal said your physical training is progressing well."

Omolewa rubbed her shoulder. "Painfully so."

"The better you become the less painful it will be," Kashta said. "You'll be struck less often. But then again, I'm not sure. Kulal is very skilled."

"Can you wrestle, *mwalimu*?"

Kashta laughed. "I have some skill, but at my age I try to avoid such confrontations. There are other responses that are much more effective."

Kashta held out his left hand then opened it. A small ball of light appeared, roiling over his palm like a ball of fire. Omolewa was fascinated.

"You will teach me to do this?"

Kashta nodded. "Large manifestations are the easiest to create. But those such as this are much more difficult because they require precision and control. They also require knowledge of the world around us and the ability to see and manipulate invisible forces and objects too small for the eyes to perceive."

"How can you move that which you cannot see?"

Kashta smiled. "That is what you will learn today. What I will share with you over the next months is information sacred to Kash. It is so valuable to our people if it was discovered I was teaching you, I and everyone in this palace would be killed."

"I'm not sure I want to learn these things," Omolewa said.

"You must," Kashta replied. "We Kashites have kept our secrets too long. All lands of Ki Khanga must share if we are to withstand the coming storm."

Here they were again, Kashta speaking of an impending event.

"And you will tell me about this storm?"

"I will. But first we must learn how to make this."

He waved his hand and the fireball dissipated.

Omolewa sat and her lessons began.

"The world consists of items large and small, things seen and unseen," Kashta said. "It is those unseen things that have the most influence on our lives. Combined with ashé and the will of Daarila and Eda, they create what we call life."

Omolewa was immediately engaged. Just those few words had sparked her interest far beyond any lessons she'd learned her entire life.

"Please, mwalimu," she said. "Continue!"

Kashta grinned and the lessons commenced.

* * *

Omolewa's mind tingled as she prepared for her afternoon ride. She halted for a moment, looking at her hands, her bed, everything. In one short lesson Kashta had altered her entire perception of her world. There were still so many questions that needed to be answered, so many theories that needed to be proven. How were these particles discovered? If one cannot see a thing, how do you know it exists? Kashta said there were ways to prove such things, some which required equipment he did not have access to beyond Kamit. It was his hope that he could prepare her enough to convince the rulers of Kamit that she should continue her studies in Kamit. This was something that had never been allowed in the entire history of the nation. To do so would be unprecedented.

The thought of traveling to yet another strange land quelled her excitement. She was still adjusting to Zimbabwa; journeying to yet another land and learning more customs and languages was not high on her mind. For now, she would concentrate on simpler things.

Omolewa was smiling as she approached the stables. Anenyasha waited, wrapped in a brown kanga.

"Your quaggat is ready," the woman said.

"Thank you," Omolewa replied.

Together they walked to Furaha's stall. The quaggat was saddled and prancing in the small space, a sign of her happiness. Omolewa opened the stall then hugged Furaha who nuzzled against her. Pik-Pik appeared in the rafters again, scampering down to the hay then to her feet. She bent down, picked her up then gave her a kiss before placing her in her riding pouch.

"You love your animals very much," Anenyasha said.

"They are my friends," Omolewa replied.

"I love animals as well. It's why I work here. The others treat them too cruelly. I try to make them feel better afterwards."

Anenyasha reached out and Furaha extended her head to her, accepting her touch. Omolewa was pleasantly surprised.

"Furaha has made another friend I see."

"She is a good quaggat. The others defer to her. It has made the stable a calmer place."

"Anenyasha, would you like to ride with us?" Omolewa asked.

The woman smiled. "I would, but I have duties."

"I will speak to my brother," Omolewa said. "I'll see if we can change your duties to accompany me on my ride."

"Are you going to ride that thing or share secrets with it?" Kulal said.

Omolewa turned to see Kulal standing with his arms folding, a frown on his face.

"Speaking of my brother," she whispered.

She twirled around with a sweet smile on her face.

"No," Kulal said.

Omolewa pouted. "You don't even know what I'm about to ask."

"It's still no."

Omolewa grasped Anenyasha's arm then pulled her close.

"I'd like Anenyasha to ride with us."

"Oh," Kulal said. "That's different. I thought it was going to be something about that quaggat."

Kulal looked at the woman and she lowered her gaze.

"Do you have any pending tasks?" he asked.

"I don't think so. I will ask Zendaya," Anenyasha replied.

She bowed then hurried away. Kulal gave Omolewa a scolding look.

"What did I do?"

"Our servants have responsibilities just like you," he said. "To interrupt them is to disturb the functions of the palace."

"It's only a ride," Omolewa said.

"You're showing your age," Kulal fussed. "Anenyasha is one of our best stable hands. It is because of her that our quaggat herd is well maintained, and as far as I know she doesn't talk to them."

Furaha snorted her disapproval and Omolewa did her best not to laugh.

"I apologize, brother," she said. "And I will apologize to Anenyasha when she returns."

Kulal's demeanor changed upon Omolewa's apology.

"It's not that serious," he confessed. "It's just that you need to learn the function and responsibilities of everyone and everything in the palace. That's the other reason you were brought here. The Dry Season Palace is a microcosm of the Central Palace. The same duties are required and expected except on a more relaxed level. It is where I became familiar with my place."

Anenyasha returned with a smile on her face.

"Zendaya has given her permission," she said.

"Good," Kulal answered. "Fetch your quaggat. We'll be waiting in the courtyard."

Anenyasha trotted away while Kulal and Omolewa exited the stable, Omolewa leading Furaha.

"There is another thing you need to be aware of," Kulal said.

"What is that?"

"Your station," he replied. "You are the daughter of the Bene. It still may not mean much to you, but to those in this palace and this land you are a very powerful person. Your favor or disfavor can make or break the lives of people. To have you as a friend can be a great advantage, especially for a servant like Anenyasha."

"What are you saying?" Omolewa asked.

"I'm saying that her feelings toward you may not be sincere," Kulal replied. "You may just be a means to an end."

Kulal's words angered her.

"You're wrong," Omolewa said. "Anenyasha is a good woman. If her intentions were false, I would know."

"You might just," Kulal said. "The full extent of your abilities has yet to be revealed. Still, it would be best to go slow with such relationships. Better yet I would advise that you avoid them altogether. The consequences could be painful and messy."

They reached the courtyard. Kulal mounted his quaggat; Omolewa hugged Furaha before climbing into her saddle.

"You speak about this as if you have some experience," Omolewa said.

Kulal nodded. "It happens to most of us sooner or later. This can be a lonely charge. Sometimes we find comfort in someone who is not of our station, someone we feel we can confide in. It usually doesn't end well."

"And who was your mistake?" she asked.

Kulal's face turned grim. "Come, we waste the day."

Anenyasha's arrival helped avoid an awkward discussion. There was another arrival as well, one that took Omolewa by surprise. She was not happy with its revelation.

"Hello, Omolewa!" Tatonga said.

"Hello, Tatonga," she replied, attempting to sound annoyed.

"My father and I arrived yesterday," he said. "I thought it best not to disturb you during your training."

"Yet you are still here," she said.

Tatonga looked embarrassed. "Yes, we are. I'll promise you you'll barely notice us. We are familiar with the palace. We can be discreet."

Anenyasha arrived on a handsome roan quaggat. She smiled at Kulal and Omolewa, but her smile faded when she looked at Tatonga. Omolewa wasn't sure, but it seemed as if Anenyasha was very upset by his presence.

Another stable hand arrived with bows and arrow-filled quivers. He handed each to the riders, including Omolewa. She looked at Kulal puzzled and he grinned.

"I said you needed to learn to hunt," he said. "Today is your first lesson."

"This was to be a relaxing ride," she replied.

"It will be, for the most part," Kulal said. "Remember, you're in training. Every event is a learning opportunity."

Tatonga rode up to her.

"I'm an excellent archer. Kulal, not so much. I would be happy to assist you."

"Thank you, Tatonga, but I think I'll rely on my brother. He is my trainer, and you are just a guest."

Tatonga's smile faded. "As you wish."

The four rode to the gate then into the forest accompanied by porters. This was not to be the ride Omolewa imagined but she would make the best of it. Kulal took the lead and the others followed, the quaggats setting a brisk pace as they travelled deeper into the forest. She sensed Furaha's pleasure as she trotted the trail. Pik-Pik stuck her head out her pouch then climbed onto her shoulders. This was exactly what they needed, time in the open. The human smells of the palace were replaced by the earthy scents of the forest and the constant chatter of wildlife. It was a scene Omolewa never experienced back home, but it was an experience she'd come to appreciate since coming to Zimbabwa.

They rode until midday. Kulal led them to a clearing beside a small river. The porters set up camp and the quaggats indulged themselves on river water and grass. Omolewa attempted to feed Pik-Pik but the ferret scampered away into the bush, apparently seeking fresher fare. With her animal companions distracted by the surroundings, Omolewa decided to spend time with her cohorts.

Kulal lay on a blanket, his head resting on his pack. Tatonga sat beside him, chewing on a grass stalk. She spotted Anenyasha sitting alone on the riverbank. Omolewa was not in the mood for Tatonga's platitudes so she joined Anenyasha by the riverside.

"May I join you?" she asked.

"Yes, *mamoyo*."

The use of her formal title annoyed Omolewa but she would follow decorum.

"Do you know this river?" she asked.

Anenyasha nodded. "We call it Munyoro. It flows south before joining with its big sister. It is a good river to fish and to swim. Not many *makarwe*.

"Makarwe?"

Anenyasha extended her arms then opened and closed them.

"Ah!" Omolewa said. "We call them *mambas* where I grew up."

"There is a place where my mama would take us to fish when I was a girl," Anenyasha said. "May I show it to you?"

"Of course."

They began to walk down the bank when Kulal's voice interrupted them.

"Don't go too far," he said. "Our meals will be ready soon."

Omolewa shook her head. Kulal was ever watchful. It was hard getting used to having an older sibling after so many years of holding the position.

"Yes, Kulal," she said, trying her best to use the tone Diwani used with her.

"Would you like me to join you?" Tatonga asked.

"No," Omolewa replied a bit too quickly. "We will we be back soon."

She glanced to see Tatonga's wounded face. She was being mean to the boy despite his efforts to be her friend. Under other circumstances she would welcome his attention, but there was too much pressure on their relationship, and she was not about to succumb to others wishes. She did not know when or if she would get married, but she was sure when she made the decision it would be with the man she chose and not for political satisfaction.

And then there was Anenyasha. This time her contempt for him was clear. She saw Omolewa look at her and attempted to mask it with a smile.

Omolewa and Anenyasha followed the winding riverbank, finally reaching a section of the river that opened into a wide pool. The waters were serving as a wading pool for a family of kibokos. They quickly made their way into the bush, careful not to disturb the aggressive and territorial behemoths.

"Kibokos," Omolewa said.

"Our name for them is mvuu," Anenyasha said. "When they are not here, this pool is a perfect place to fish. It is also a good hunting ground, since so many animals come here to drink."

"We should keep this to ourselves," Omolewa said.

"I'm sure Kulal knows of it," Anenyasha replied. "He is a very good hunter and knows the bush well."

"Still, we will say nothing."

"As you wish, mamoyo."

"Anenyasha, why do you hate Tatonga?"

"I don't hate him," Anenyasha answered. "I don't know him."

"I see the look on your face,' Omolewa said.

"I tend not to like people when I first meet them," she explained. "It is my way."

"Did you feel the same towards me?"

Anenyasha shook her head and smiled. "You are different. You displayed your kindness in how you cared for your animals. I had no time to hate you."

Omolewa laughed.

"Fair enough."

They enjoyed the quietness for a time then returned to the camp. The porters were serving the meal and the two of them took their bowls and joined everyone. Once the meal was complete Kulal stood.

"We'll hunt north of here," he said. "There is a path used by bush deer and pigs that leads to a nearby waterhole. If we are lucky, we may enjoy either for dinner tonight."

"I hope we're lucky," Tatonga replied. "I don't relish eating smoked meat again."

The porters brought Omolewa her bow and quiver. She handled the weapon as if it was a foreign object.

"I think someone might need a little bit of practice before we set out," Tatonga said.

"I can show her," Anenyasha replied.

"Really?" Tatonga looked surprised. "When does a stable hand have time to hunt?"

"I hunted often as a young woman. Before I came to work for the Bene."

"Care to show us your skill?" Tatonga asked.

"Am I allowed?" Anenyasha asked Kulal.

"Yes," he said. "But if Tatonga is asking, Tatonga should make it worth your while."

"That is not necessary," Anenyasha said.

"I don't mind at all," Tatonga said. "I will choose a target. If you can hit it three times, I'll pay you a month's wages."

Anenyasha's eyes went wide. "That is too generous."

"Not at all," Kulal said. "What do you want if he loses, Tatonga?"

"She will return with us and become my stable master."

Anenyasha smiled. "I'm not sure if I should win or lose."

Tatonga smiled. "That's exactly the point."

Anenyasha took her bow and quiver.

"Choose the target," she said.

"That," Tatonga said as he pointed.

Tatonga chose a sapling so thin it swayed with the slight breeze. Omolewa became upset.

"That's not fair, Tatonga!" she said.

"It is fine, mamoyo," Anenyasha replied.

The woman loaded the bow then took aim. She hummed as she looked at the sapling then let the arrow fly. It struck the sapling.

"Excellent!" Kulal shouted.

"It's not over yet," Tatonga said. "She has to hit it twice more."

"The fact that she hit it once is good enough as far as I'm concerned," Kulal replied.

"Me, too," Omolewa added.

"This only shows she's held a bow before," Tatonga commented. "Anyone can get lucky."

Anenyasha loaded the bow then shot again. The arrow struck the sapling near its base. Kulal raised his hands in mock surrender.

"I'm convinced," he said.

"One more shot," Tatonga said.

Anenyasha took careful aim. She drew the bow, then turned toward Tatonga and let the arrow loose. The arrow sank into his throat, and he collapsed.

"Now!" she shouted.

Dozens of warriors surged from the forest and rushed from the other side of the river. Kulal attempted to raise his hands but was struck on the head by a thrown club. He fell the ground and was immediately set upon. The warriors tied his hands, gagged him then threw a bag over his head. Omolewa stood stunned, the entire scene unfolding before her like a nightmare. She turned to face Anenyasha. The woman expression was sorrowful despite having just murdered Tatonga.

"I'm sorry, mamoyo," she said.

Omolewa felt a dull pain at the back of her head and the world went dark.

- 1 1 -

Omolewa awoke shrouded in darkness. Her head throbbed, the pain emanating from where she'd been struck. She wasn't blindfolded yet she could not see. She tried to move her hands and discovered they were tied behind her back. Omolewa attempted to use her ashé to free herself. She concentrated on the ropes around her hand, trying to visualize the knot but the pain in her head wouldn't allow her to focus. A wave of hopelessness swept over her, and tears came to her eyes. The emotion was quickly replaced by anger. She cursed the day Kulal stepped into their lives. But it was not her brother's fault. The guilt lay in the Bene's hands. It was she who sent him. She was the one who summoned her into this life, attempting to mold her into something she never wanted to be. She had gone along with it hoping that by doing so she would bring a better life to her family. But that was not to be. She had no idea who her captives were and what they intended to do with her, but she knew she would never see her family or Nacala again.

"She's awake," a gruff voice said.

Rough hands gripped her arms then lifted her to a sitting position. Omolewa didn't resist; she would play along until she knew what was afoot. Those same hands pulled her to her feet then lifted her onto someone's shoulder. She was carried from wherever she had been into sunlight which hurt her eyes. Her porter placed her down onto what felt like grass. She heard the waterfall before she saw it; the people standing before her came into focus moments later. Anenyasha stood beside a tall woman wearing a towering headdress which made her appear even more formidable. A man stood on the opposite side, his broad body covered with leather armor. He held a spear in his right hand; his left hand rested on the hilt of his sheathed sword. Sitting next to him was Kulal. Her brother was gagged and bound. Whatever else they had done to him rendered his ashé useless as well. Anenyasha noticed her gaze then looked away.

"Untie her," the woman said.

Anenyasha tipped toward her. She stepped behind Omolewa then untied her.

"I'm sorry," she said.

"Don't speak to me!" Omolewa spat.

"Do not blame Anenyasha for her actions," the woman said. "She did what she was ordered to do."

"She murdered Tatonga!" Omolewa shouted.

"That boy was not your friend, neither was his father," the man replied.

"And I am supposed to believe you? I don't even know who you are."

"We are an interested party," the woman said.

"What does that mean?"

The woman stepped toward Omolewa. Omolewa raised her hands, read to use what Kashta had taught her thus far. Her head pain had subsided, and she felt her ashé.

"See," the man said. "She's been trained."

The woman came closer. "I'm sure she has some skills. The Bene would not have sent for her otherwise. But she's only been with them a few weeks. She can only be…"

Omolewa thrust her hands toward the woman, lifting her and the others into the air. She was about to drop them into the water behind them, but something prevented her from doing so. A smirk on the woman's face told Omolewa what the something was.

"Release us," the woman said.

"No," Omolewa replied.

The woman gestured and Omolewa's grip on them loosened. She gritted her teeth and it tightened again. The woman's smirk was replaced by concern.

"Release us." This time her statement was a plea.

"There are things you need to know before you return to the palace," she continued. "Things that will save your life and the lives of your family."

"I will not let you go," Omolewa said. Her grip was weakening, her ashé affected by her own physical weakness. "Who are you?"

"They are the Mungwe," Kulal said. Omolewa looked toward her brother. He was still gagged and bound and seemed to be unconscious, yet she heard his voice. She was about to speak to him, but he cut her off.

"No. Just listen. These are the people we fought long ago, the reason you were sent away. They have a powerful sonchai. We thought they had fled Zimbabwa long ago, but we were wrong. They have come to reclaim what they think is theirs. Do not believe anything they say."

"Why should I believe the words of the Mungwe?" Omolewa said.

The woman grinned. "You know more than we suspected. Then we must be truthful in all things. The first is that while you are skilled, I know you can't hold us much longer. As a gesture of our sincerity, I will not kill you once your strength fails."

Omolewa kept her fear from showing in her expression. Her arms shook as she attempted to keep her spiritual grip on the group.

"If you truly wish to show your good will, free my brother," Omolewa said.

The woman nodded. "So be it."

Kulal's bonds unraveled; the blindfold lifted from his eyes. He stirred then sat up, holding his head for a moment before slowly rising to his feet. He shared a weak grin with Omolewa.

"Let them go," he said.

"Are you sure?" Omolewa asked.

"Yes" Kulal replied. "Any sonchai who could release me while you held her in your grip could have hurt you long ago."

Kulal looked at the sonchai then nodded. The woman nodded back. Omolewa eased her arms down and the

Mungwe descended to the ground. No sooner after she let them go did she sit on the ground herself, exhausted.

The sonchai walked toward them, a solemn look on her face.

"Thank you for your wisdom," she said. "I am Bunjiwe Ndelu. I represent my people in this matter. We apologize for our method; if we had come to you any other way we would have been thwarted."

"Did you have to kill Tatonga?" Kulal asked. For the first time since his friend's death Omolewa heard emotion in his voice.

"That which you saw was not your friend," Bunjiwe replied. "Tatonga and his family are not who you remember them to be. They have been converted by forces that are focused on your destruction. Thus is the power of the threat we face."

"The Joka Watu?" Kulal asked.

Bunjiwe nodded her head. "Do you remember the staff Tatonga's father showed you?"

"Yes," Kulal said. "But how did you know of this?"

"That does not matter. That staff was a symbol of their conversion. To follow the gods of Menu-Kash is to serve the Joka-Watu. The wheels are in motion; the people of the Cleave are prepared to Rupture. We must go to the palace and speak to the Kamite."

"You know about mwalimu Kashta?" Omolewa said.

"I did not know his name, but I was aware of his presence," Bunjiwe replied. "A man possessing such power cannot walk among those with our sight and not be sensed. But we have wasted enough time. We must go to the palace immediately. If Tatonga has come, his father is not far behind."

The warrior stuck his fingers into his mouth then whistled. A herd of riding beasts appeared, those of which Omolewa was unfamiliar with. The quaggats were among them as well. Furaha ran up to Omolewa then nuzzled her. She seemed comfortable among the animals, sturdy goat-like creatures that seemed bred for the mountainous environment.

Kulal hesitated. "I'm still not sure I believe you. The Joka Watu have attacked us before so I would not be surprised if they have attempted to infiltrate Zimbabwa. But Tatonga? He was my best friend!"

Omolewa sensed Kulal building his ashé and she was sure Bunjiwe sensed it as well. The woman made no gestures to defend herself.

"I would have preferred to capture your friend and force him to reveal his true intentions, but we have no time. I sense that you have considerable strength Kulal, and if forced I will hurt you. I hope it doesn't come to that."

"You may be able to defeat me, but I doubt if you can defeat us both," Kulal said. He looked at Omolewa and nodded. Omolewa looked at Bunjiwe. The woman's expression was stoic.

"Kulal, I don't think we should…"

"It doesn't matter what you think!" Kulal blurted. "We are family, and we stand together. This woman is Mungwe. They are the reason you were sent away. They are the reason our father is dead!"

"You speak with emotion," Bunjiwe said. "Try to listen to reason."

"You killed my friend," Kulal said. "I need no reason."

The drum voices cut through the trees despite their distance from the Dry Season palace. Kulal's eyes went wide.

"The palace is under attack!"

"Tatonga's father is here," Bunjiwe said. "He has come for you both."

Kulal jumped on his quaggat then galloped away. Omolewa mounted Furaha. She looked at Bunjiwe.

"Will you help us?" she asked.

"No," the woman said. "We will not interfere where we are not wanted. Sometimes we must learn hard lessons. If you survive, return to this place."

"How will I know the way?"

The woman smiled. "Furaha knows."

Omolewa's eyes went wide. "How did you…"

"Go," Bunjiwe said. "Your brother needs you."

Furaha leapt forward then plunged into the bush. Omolewa knew she was swift, but she wasn't aware how fast the quaggat could run. In moments they were behind Kulal, following him through the bush. Both beasts seemed to know the way, dodging through the brush until they reached the road. Their speed increased as they crossed familiar ground, the call of the drums clear. Smoke rose over the trees as fearful and angry voices reached their ears. There was a flash that resembled lightning. Whatever had come to the palace was being confronted by Kashta.

They rounded a tight curve and were stunned at what they saw. A gaping ragged hole replaced the palace gate, rubble strewn on either side of the breach. The quaggats rushed in without hesitation; Omolewa flinched as she saw the bodies of the rampart guards. She broke her eyes away from the unfortunate warriors to a sight that filled her with dread and caused her to gasp. A giant being stood in the center of the courtyard surrounded by the meager occupants, turning its stone head from side to side as the archers fired upon it. Their arrows bounced from its body as it advanced, each footfall gouging the soft earth and destroying everything in its path. There was a bright flash before it then a sound that resembled thunder. The giant shook then staggered back, almost falling from the shock of the blast.

"Kashta!" Kulal shouted. He reined his horse then jumped to the ground.

Omolewa followed her brother toward the behemoth. Her body trembled in fear; never had she seen such a thing.

"Omolewa!"

Kulal's voice shook her. She looked to her brother in desperation.

"What do we do?" she pleaded.

"Gather everything you have," he said. "Release it on my signal."

Omolewa closed her eyes then concentrated on her center. She felt the warmth form inside her. Her eyes tightened and her muscles when rigid as she built the energy into a burning ball. Sweat formed on her forehead mark; she felt as if she stood in the center of a raging fire. She looked at Kulal;

his eyes glowing from the energy he held inside. He looked at her, nodded, and then looked toward the stone giant advancing on Kashta.

"Now!" Kulal shouted.

Omolewa unleashed her energy. Bright blue light streamed from her hands, her eyes and her mouth. The power from her body intertwined with Kulal's, striking the giant in the center of its back. But instead of blasting the giant, the energy was dispersed throughout its body. The giant stood still as it absorbed their power and grew larger. Omolewa fell to her knees, her energy momentarily spent, her hope giving way to despair. They had not hurt the beast. They had made it stronger.

The giant flashed like a thundercloud. Tendrils of energy shot in every direction, striking the men and women of the palace with equal fury. Omolewa was blinded as a bolt struck her, lifting her off her feet then slamming her into the ground. She recovered quickly, scrambling to her feet. She looked for Kulal and found him sprawled nearby. His body was still.

"Kulal!"

Omolewa ran to her brother then knelt by his side. He breathed, yet barely. The ground shook; Omolewa turned to see the giant stalking toward her. That could only mean that Kashta fared no better than Kulal. At worst, the mwalimu was dead.

"Go," Kulal whispered. "You are not strong enough to defeat it by yourself."

"I'll help you," Omolewa said.

"No," he replied. "Go!"

Furaha appeared at her side as if summoned. She took a long look at Kulal before jumping onto the quaggat.

"Run like you've never run in your life," she whispered.

The quaggat bounded for the wall. Omolewa sensed energy rising around her. She looked back and saw the giant glowing, building its power for another release. She knew this bolt would be for her and Furaha. She kept her eye on the creature as it reached its peak. At the moment she sensed it, she pulled Furaha's reins back, bringing the quaggat to a halt. Her effort was half successful. The energy stream streaked beyond them like an errant spear, but they were still too close. The blast sent them both flying. Omolewa struck the ground hard, gasping for breath. Furaha tumbled away then scrambled to its feet. Instinctive fear took over the beast and it ran from the castle into the forest.

Omolewa clambered over the wall rumble then plunged into the forest, hoping the dense foliage would conceal her. The colossus marched after her, crushing the forest with its massive feet. The palace burned behind it, the flickering flame light dispersing the dusk. Omolewa scrambled up a steep hill, but she knew her efforts were fruitless. She could not outrun this thing. She had watched it kill Kashta and possibly Kulal. There was no running from it. She would have to face it.

She turned toward the amalgam of rock and earth, her eyes narrowing as she marshaled her depleted ashé. Omolewa ripped whole trees from the ground then flung them at the thing. Some hit their mark; others were shattered by its arm-like appendages. She slowed it, but she could not stop it. Just as she was about to give into her anguish, she remembered the recent lessons of Kashta, and a smile came to her. She could not defeat this beast from without. She would have to do so from within.

Omolewa concentrated on the giant. She felt its rough surface, the stones and wood and decayed flesh pressed into form then animated by some internal power. She went inward, seeing particles of dust, small animal-like things that thrived oblivious to the form they resided in. She pressed deeper, observing particles common to the living and the lifeless arranged in patterns that gave them substance and bonded by forces which revealed themselves as light. This was what she sought. This was what she had to do to stop the colossus. Omolewa poured all she had into the being, grasping the bonds that held the particles together then yanking them apart. At the last moment she realized her triumph and her mistake then braced for the consequences. There was no sound; a light brighter than a dozen suns appeared where the colossus had been, speeding toward her at an incredible pace, burning all in its path. An invisible force reached her before the burning light, hitting her and lifting her off her feet. Her ashé encased her instinctively, protecting her from the violent force and searing heat as the world around her burned. Omolewa did not feel her body crashing into the ashes. She was unconscious when the light faded, leaving charred destruction in its wake. Rain pattered her face, reviving her. She sat up then immediately grabbed her throbbing head with her soiled hands. She eventually opened her eyes to see the destruction she had wrought. The colossus was gone, but so was everything else as far as she could see. Whatever she had done went far beyond anything she had imagined.

Omolewa stood then swayed, her weak legs. She sought a stick or branch to steady herself but there was nothing but ashes surrounding her. Despite her feebleness she had to return to the palace. She limped toward the gray walls, shuffling through the thick layer of ash. Halfway to the wall she came across a small crater. Inside the depression was the body of a man. Omolewa peered into the pit; it was Tatonga's father. He had been the core of the colossus. Why he remained intact while everything around her was destroyed she did not know. Whatever his condition, she was sure he would still be in his open grave when she returned.

She heard the distressed voices of the survivors as she reached the walls. People ran to and fro extinguishing fires with dirt and water and tending to the injured. She saw Kulal sitting upright, a woman wrapping his arm with bandages. Furaha sat nearby him, shaking her head. She made her way toward Kulal.

"Mamoyo!" someone shouted. A host of survivors surged toward her, looks of relief and joy on their faces. They crowded around her, their babbling unintelligible to her. She finally reached Kulal; her brother stood, and they hugged, both of them crying.

"I thought you were dead!" he said.

"I thought the same of you," she replied.

The woman tending Kulal touched his shoulder.

"Nevanji, you must sit," she said.

Kulal eased to the ground, pulling Omolewa with him.

"What did you do out there?" he asked her.

"I'm not sure," Omolewa replied.

"I've never seen anything like that. Kashta was right about you. You are special."

The look in Kulal's eyes disturbed her. It was a look of respect and admiration she did not deserve, especially from her brother.

"Bunjiwe was right," Omolewa said. "It was Tatonga's father, which means what she said about Tatonga was true, also."

Kulal dropped his forehead into his hands.

"Where is Kashta?" she asked.

Kulal's face became solemn.

"No!"

Omolewa ran to where she last saw her mwalimu. A group of servants milled about, their heads low. Omolewa pushed through the gathering. Kashta lay before her, his clothes and body badly burned. Omolewa knelt beside his body, covering her face as she prayed.

"May your spirit find its way home to rest among your ancestors," she said. It was as simple prayer, yet it conveyed all she felt in her heart.

"What do we do, Mamoyo?" one of the servants asked.

"Wrap his body," Omolewa replied. "We will take it back with us."

With Kashta dead and Kulal injured, the servants and warriors looked to Omolewa for instructions. She did what she thought mama and baba would do. The fires were extinguished; she sent servants to search the palace and take a census of who survived and who did not. Fortunately, most survived by seeking shelter in the recesses of the palace. It also helped that she and Kulal had arrived not long after the giant breached the walls. Still, too many had died because of Tatonga and his father's deception.

It was almost nightfall when the Mungwe arrived. They entered the palace tentatively, following the sonchai whose outstretched arms and open hands were a gesture of peace. Still, the remaining guards approached them with weapons drawn. None of them were old enough to be veterans of the old war, but all of them were raised on the stories.

Omolewa and Kulal met the Mungwe at the entrance.

"I see you have defeated the threat," Bunjiwe said.

"For now," Omolewa replied.

"You must return to the main palace immediately," the sonchai said. "There will be more attacks and they will be more numerous. The Mungwe and Zimbabwans must work together to survive."

Bunjiwe reached into her robes then extracted an object. It was a necklace, a large blue stone encircled by silver attached to a golden chain. She draped it over Omolewa's head and Omolewa immediately sensed its ashé.

"Show this to the Bene as a token of our sincerity," Bunjiwe said.

"What is it?" Omolewa asked.

"Kipande," Kulal replied. "A rare and precious thing. Created by Daarila when he struck Ki Khanga with his axe."

Kulal looked at Bunjiwe.

"How did you come across such a thing?" he asked.

"That is our secret," Bunjiwe answered.

The sonchai leaned close to Omolewa then whispered in her ear.

"Do not let the Bene have it, no matter what she says. It evens things between the two of you."

Omolewa was puzzled. She drew away from the sonchai.

"Evens things?"

Bunjiwe's face became somber. "You will see."

Bunjiwe stepped back among her entourage.

"We will leave you now," she said.

"You could help us," Kulal said.

A sad smile came to Bunjiwe's face.

"There are many among my people who do not agree with what I do," she said. "Like you, they still see us as enemies. So, this is as much as we can do for now. Talk to your mother. What happens between our people in the future depends on her."

The Mungwe left the palace then disappeared into the bush. The palace guard commander appeared no sooner had the last Mungwe entered the forest.

"Do you wish us to pursue them, nevanji?" he asked.

"No," Kulal replied. "As they say we have much to do here. Secure the palace as well as you can. We're leaving."

"As you wish, nevanji," the commander replied.

"And send a rider to the Central palace immediately," Kulal continued. "Let them know what happened here."

"Immediately, nevanji," the commander said.

Kulal looked at Omolewa.

"Come help me," he said.

"Do what?" she asked.

"Heal the others."

"I don't know how to do that," Omolewa said. "Kashta never had the chance to teach me healing. I don't know which herbs to use."

"You don't need herbs," Kulal said. "You have that."

He pointed at the necklace.

"But I don't know . . ."

"You have to try. For them."

Kulal extended his injured arm.

"You can try me first."

Omolewa took Kulal's arm. He winced when she moved it and she jerked her hands away.

"It's okay," Kulal said.

Omolewa took his arm again. She looked at it on the surface; his skin darkened where his arm was injured. She closed her eyes then used the inward sight Kashta taught her. She saw the damaged muscle and bone. His arm wasn't broken, but it was deeply bruised.

"I can see your wound," she said.

"Good. Now fix it."

Omolewa opened her eyes.

"I told you Kashta didn't teach me!"

"Focus on the kipande Bunjiwe gave you," he said. "It will know."

Omolewa took Kulal's arm once more. She focused on his wound again, but is time she also focused on the warm stone pressed against her chest. She switched her focus between the two, waiting for something, anything to happen. When it did it, caught her by surprised. There was a flash in her mind like lighting. The flash became a visible strand of light; her mind the conduit between the kipande and Kulal's wound. She watched with her small eye as the damage tissue transformed, resembling the undamaged flesh. The bone altered as well, the bone fragments migrating back into place then fusing into the surrounding bone. The current diminished as the wound healed. The connection broke and Omolewa was swept by a wave of fatigue that caused her to stumble. The servants steadied her then helped her sit.

Kulal moved his arm about then grinned.

"You did it!" he exclaimed.

"I guess I did," she replied. "It was like you said. But I am very tired."

"We will do what we can," Kulal said. "I only ask that you help with the more seriously wounded."

"I will try," Omolewa said.

They worked throughout the night, finding survivors and gathering provisions for the long trip back to the Central Palace. Omolewa performed a few more healings, but she finally had to refuse any more. She fell to sleep totally exhausted; when she awoke it was still night. Kulal sat beside her, a look of relief on his face.

"I'm sorry," she said. "I didn't mean to fall asleep. I feel better now. Let's continue."

"There's no need," he said. "Everything is packed. We'll leave in the morning."

"That was very fast," she said. "I thought it would take at least three days."

"It did," Kulal said. "You slept for two days."

Omolewa sat up straight, her hand grasping the necklace.

"That is not all," Kulal said.

He handed Omolewa a mirror then held up a torch. She saw her face then gasped, almost dropping the mirror.

Fine wrinkles emanated from the corners of her eyes and a patch of her hair had turned white. She took the necklace from around her neck then threw it as far as she could.

"Get that thing away from me!" she shouted before she began to cry.

"Fetch the necklace," Kulal said to one of the servants. He sat beside Omolewa and put his arm around her. She shrugged it away.

"This is your fault!" she said. "You told me to do this."

"I didn't know there would be consequences. But I should have. Daarila does not share his power without a price. That is how he and Eda differ."

"That does not help me now," she said between sobs.

"Don't worry," he said. "Maybe the change is temporary."

Omolewa glared at her brother. "And if it's not?"

"Them maybe mama can help you," Kulal said. "Or you should pray to Eda."

Omolewa looked in the mirror again. This time she didn't cry. This was it, she thought. She took the box from the servant then put the necklace back on. Twice she had done something in order help and in the process caused herself harm.

She did not sleep that night, her mind filled with morbid thoughts. As the sun rose, she hurried to the stables. Furaha was waiting when she opened the stall, trotting to her then snuggling against her. Pik-Pik appeared as well, curling around her next and nipping playfully at her ear. The animals relaxed her as they vied for her attention.

"What is happening to me?" she said to them. "I don't want this. I don't want any of this."

When she finally emerged from the stable, she was calm but still unnerved. Kulal greeted her hesitantly.

"How are you?" he asked.

"I'm well," she answered.

"Good. We are ready to depart. You and I will lead."

Omolewa nodded. She saddled Furaha then mounted. She rode out to the other others; the wounded were secured in wagons and the guard mounted. Those without horses walked alongside the wagons and the riders. They filed out the damaged gate and began their journey back to the Central Palace. Omolewa turned for one last look at the broken citadel. She would always remember it as the place where she finally decided who she would be. She turned away and focused on the journey ahead.

- 1 2 -

One week after leaving the Dry Season palace the outriders met the beleaguered party. Omolewa rode at the rear of their group, her mind blank from the monotonous pace. A spirited commotion from ahead conveyed their arrival; moments later a Zimbabwan warrior galloped up to her, his lance held at his side and worried look on his face.

"Mamoyo, are you okay?" he said.

"I am fine," Omolewa replied. "Please see to the wounded. They have been a long time without care."

"We will, mamoyo," he answered. "Immediately."

Though the sight of the warrior was a relief, it was the second person riding toward her that filled her heart with joy.

"Baba!" she cried.

Baba rode toward her dressed as a Zimbabwan warrior, a wide smile of his face. They dismounted simultaneously and Omolewa ran into his arms. The emotions she held inside for the past few days spilled from her eyes, her tears staining baba's shirt.

"We were so worried about you," he said. "When the outrider appeared at the palace and told us what happened I was the first to prepare. Your mother wanted to come too, but we did not know what we might find when we met with you. It took me a long time to convince her to stay."

Omolewa looked up at her father and smiled.

"So much has happened," she said. "So much has changed."

Baba's smile faded.

"What happened to you?" he asked.

"I did something to save us," she said. "This was the result."

Baba's smile slowly returned.

"It will be okay," he said. "The Bene has asked that you be brought to her as soon as you arrive," he said. "Maybe she can help. What do you wish to do?"

Baba spoke to her as if they had a choice.

"I wish to see her," Omolewa said. "I have something to give her."

"What is that?" baba asked, his eyes on the necklace around her neck.

"It was given to me by the Mungwe," Omolewa said.

The mention of the Mungwe made baba's eyes widen.

"You should get rid of it," baba said. "You know who the Mungwe are, don't you?"

Omolewa nodded.

"Then you should know that they cannot be trusted," baba said. "That is kipande, is it not?"

"Yes," Omolewa answered.

"That alone makes it dangerous."

Baba stared at her, as if seeing her for the first time.

"Have you used it?"

Omolewa touched the patch of white hair over her forehead.

"Yes."

"So that's the culprit." Baba reached for the necklace and Omolewa turned away.

"Give it to me," he said.

"No," Omolewa replied.

"Give it to me!" he shouted.

Baba lunged at Omolewa. She jerked her hand upward; baba slammed into an invisible barrier, the force knocking him to the ground. He looked up at Omolewa in shock.

"You…you struck me?"

Omolewa immediately regretted her actions. She knelt beside her baba.

"I'm sorry baba," she said. "But I am tired of the Bene, and I do not trust her. I think she wants more from me than she lets on."

"I don't know what has happened that would make you strike me and disobey me," Baba said, ignoring her words. "What have the Mungwe done to you?"

"They have done nothing to me," Omolewa replied. "Since the day I met Kulal I've been led to believe that all this was for my benefit. That being the Bene's daughter would be the perfect life which I deserved. But Kulal did not come for me to make our lives better. The Bene has other plans."

Baba stood, keeping his distance from Omolewa. She noticed his apprehension and sadness swept over her.

"Who did you talk to that makes you doubt the Bene?"

"Bunjiwe," Kulal said.

Her brother joined her.

"What the Mungwe sonchai said made sense," he continued. "As much as I love my mama, I too am wary of her motives. The Mungwe helped us. They parleyed with us without any hint of violence. All that they ask is that Omolewa talk to mama and warn her of a pending threat."

"And what threat is that?" Baba asked.

"The shadows that has been hovering over us since we left Nacala," Kulal said. "The Joka Watu."

"We won't solve anything here," Baba said. "The sooner we get back to the palace the better. Then we can meet with the Bene and sort things out."

"I agree," Kulal said.

He rode away to the lead of the column.

Baba watched Kulal ride away then glared at Omolewa.

"Never strike me again," he said.

"I won't, baba," she replied.

Baba's stare gave way to a smile.

"It's not like I could stop you anyway," he said. "If you won't do it again out of fear, at least humor me out of respect."

Omolewa laughed, the first time she'd done so in days."

"I would never hurt your baba," she said. "Never."

"I know you wouldn't, Lewa," he answered.

190

"When do I see mama, Diwani and Kazija?"

"They will be at the palace with the Bene," baba said.

Omolewa stomach churned with worry. She did not know how the Bene would receive her and she didn't want her family nearby if it was not pleasant.

"I was hoping to have some private time with you before seeing her."

"We wanted the same, but the Bene was insistent. You can understand her worry after the message we received. The city is on high alert. Warriors patrol the streets, and the palace guard has been doubled."

"I see," Omolewa said. Her hand went to the necklace. It seems she would have to deal with the Bene sooner than she imagined.

As they entered the city boundaries baba's words were confirmed. The roads teemed with warriors, some marching in columns, others on riding quaggats. The numbers around them grew until they resembled a small army riding toward the Central Palace. Archers filled the ramparts, supported by spearmen pacing the stone walkways. The city was prepared for war. Omolewa tensed as she rode through the gates. She could fell the apprehension in Furaha as well. Pik-Pik chattered in her ear, expression her agitation.

"I know," she whispered. "Nothing is the same. Not even me."

They dismounted at the palace entrance then followed the guard to the Meeting hall, Omolewa's anxiety increasing with each step. As the doors to the hall opened, she fought against panic. Soothing warmth spread across her chest then her body, emanating from the amulet. The Bene sat on her stool, flanked by her guards. Omolewa saw mama, Diwani and Kazija and waved. Her joy was cut short by a shriek that cut through the room.

The cry came from the Bene. She sprang from her stood then marched toward Omolewa, her eyes focused on the amulet.

"Where did you get that?" she shouted.

"I . . ."

"Give it to me now!"

The Bene reached out with her hand and her power to take the amulet. Once again Omolewa's response was instinctive. She covered the amulet with her hands while throwing up the barrier that thwarted her father. The Bene wasn't as easily denied. Omolewa felt the Bene's ashé piercing her shield like a million needles. She used her small sight as Kashta taught her, closing the gaps and smashing the Bene's penetration. She was tempted to use the kipande's power, but the image of her white hair stopped her. She would resist the Bene on her own.

The Bene pulled back.

"Everyone leave us," she ordered. "Now!"

The warriors and elders vacated the room. Kulal remained, standing between Omolewa and the Bene, his eyes shifting between mother and sister. Omolewa's family gathered around her. Her mother and siblings looked fearful; baba looked defiant, his hand on his sword.

Omolewa spoke to them without taking her eyes off the Bene.

"You must leave," she said. "All of you."

"We won't leave you alone," Baba said.

"Don't stay for me," Omolewa replied. "Leave for Diwani and Kazija."

She looked at baba and he understood the meaning of the words.

"She won't do it," baba said.

"I don't know what she'll do," Omolewa replied. "Please mama and baba. Go."

Diwani ran to her then hugged her waist.

"No, no, no, no!" he cried.

Kazija tried to reach her, but mama swept her up.

"Come now," she said. Tears streamed from her eyes as she looked at Omolewa.

Baba pried Diwani from her then picked him up. He struggled hard against baba's grip.

"No!" he screamed.

Baba caught up with Mama and they hurried from the room. The Bene said nothing; her eyes transfixed on the amulet.

"Who gave it to you?" she asked, her voice almost a whisper.

"Bunjiwe, the Mungwe sonchai," Omolewa answered.

"So, she is still alive," the Bene said.

"She sent it as a peace offering," Omolewa said.

The Bene laughed. "She sent it to taunt me. She is no fool. Giving the amulet to you makes you my enemy, or so she hopes."

"That is not true," Kulal said. "Our enemy is the Joka Watu."

"Did she tell you who the amulet used to belong to?" The Bene asked.

Omolewa became uneasy. "No. She did not."

The Bene smiled. "It belonged to her brother; your father."

Omolewa was stunned, but not as much as Kulal. His eyes went wide then his expression darkened.

"So, it is true," he said. "You killed him. You killed our baba!"

Omolewa felt the Bene's ashé shift from her to Kulal. Before he could raise his hands, she struck him. He fell to the ground. Omolewa sensed he was still alive.

"Yes, I killed him," the Bene said as she gazed at Kulal's limp form. "I killed him because he betrayed me."

She shifted her eyes back to Omolewa.

"The war we fought when you were born was against the Mungwe. Your baba was Mungwe; our marriage was arranged in order to bring peace between our people. As a symbol of unity, we were given the Twins, two amulets possessing the power of kipande. You wear his; I have not worn mine since his death."

"If your marriage was to bring peace, what happened?" Omolewa asked.

"Some people are never faithful to their words," the Bene replied. "They live to lie. I did not love your baba when we first married, nor did he love me. Our love grew over time, at least mine did. I thought the birth of Kulal would bring us closer, but it did not. When you were born, I hoped again, but I was wrong. Soon afterwards a new war broke out between our people. I tried to remain neutral and work toward peace, but your baba had chosen to secretly support his own. He gave his amulet to Bunjiwe to aid her. I discovered this after we sent you away. In my fury I lost control of my powers and I…I killed him."

Omolewa braced herself. She could feel the Bene's emotions but could not discern which one would rule her actions. The Bene looked at her and Omolewa could tell she sensed the same.

"I don't want to fight you," she said. "There has been enough disappointment in my life. I hoped we would be close when you returned but I know now that you were away too long. You will never see me as you see the woman who raised you, nor will you ever love us as much as you love them. That is lost to us. But we don't need to be adversaries."

"I never wanted any of this," Omolewa replied. "In the beginning it was all intoxicating. To find out that you are the daughter of the Bene, that you possess ashé, that you have a family beyond your own; it was exciting. But this war, the Joka Watu; I don't want to be a part of this. I'm not ready for this."

The Bene stepped toward her. Omolewa felt her ashé subside, but she kept her guard up.

"It is like Kashta told you. We don't get to choose our roles in the plans of the ancestors. All we can do is play them. And you have a very important role. No matter how you feel, you are my daughter and sooner or later you will have to answer to your responsibility."

The Bene knelt beside Kulal then lifted his head onto her lap.

"My son would do anything for me before you came," she said. "You changed him as you have changed me. I'm not sure what the Mungwe are up to, but I don't fear them. I will meet with Bunjiwe and determine if their overtures are sincere."

"And what of me?" Omolewa asked.

The Bene looked up then smiled.

"Go home, Omolewa," she said. "Go back to Nacala."

Joy swept throughout Omolewa.

"Do you mean this?" she asked. "You will not try to stop me?"

"Yes, I mean it, and I won't stop you. I can see you are determined to leave, and the only way I can stop you would mean making you my enemy."

The Bene stroked Kulal's hair. "I am tired of fighting my family. Whatever Zimbabwa faces, I will deal with it alone."

She looked at Omolewa and for the first time since she came to Zimbabwa she sensed true emotion from the Bene.

"I see a part of me in you," the Bene said. "You are smart and determined. Yet you love much better than I do. Go and hold your family close as long as you can. But remember that you cannot escape your fate. One day I will call on you and you must answer."

Omolewa barely heard the Bene's last words. She ran from the chamber, bursting through the doors where her family waited.

"We're going home!" she shouted. "We're going home!"

She rushed her family, trying her best to hug them all at once.

"What a minute," baba said. "What do you mean we're going home? This is our home now."

"No, it's not," Omolewa said. "It never was, and it never will be. The Bene said we can go back to Nacala!"

Mama's worry showed on her face.

"She is allowing this?" she asked.

Omolewa's face became serious.

"She cannot stop it."

Baba's expression changed as Omolewa uttered those words. There was fear in his eyes, fear of her. It was not the emotion she wished from him, but she understood why he felt that way. She was different now. Even she did not know what that would mean in the future.

"Come," mama said. "Let's gather our things as soon as possible. I've had enough of Zimbabwa. I want my family back."

Together they hurried down the hall to their rooms.

- 1 3 -

The monsoons blew north, pushing wisps of white clouds across the crystal blue skies. Omolewa stood on the deck of the dhow, Pik-Pik scurrying about in his pouch at her waist while Kazija squirmed in her arms. She grinned as her little sister did her best to break free.

"Put me down!" she fussed. "I want to run!"

"Not yet, mouse," Omolewa replied. "The deck hands have much to do before we launch, and you'll get in the way."

"No, I won't," Kazija replied. "I'll help them. I'm strong!"

She rolled her little fingers into fist then bent her arms to display the biceps that didn't exist.

"Be patient or I'll feed you to Pik-Pik," Omolewa said.

Kazija squeaked then buried her face into Omolewa's shoulder.

"That was mean to say. Feeding your sister to a ferret?"

Omolewa turned to see Kulal sauntering toward her, his warm smile stirring regrets.

"So, you decided to come," she said.

"I had to see you off," he replied. "Can't let my only sister leave without saying goodbye."

He kissed her cheek then took her chin in his hand.

"What?" she asked.

"Your wrinkles are fading," he said.

"I know," Omolewa said. "But the white hair remains. It's a warning, I think."

"Eda only knows," Kulal said. He hugged her again and she smiled. She would miss his hugs.

"This is not a happy day for me, or for Zimbabwa," he said.

"You and Zimbabwa will be okay," Omolewa replied.

"I don't know," Kulal lowered his head. "You were the only person that didn't look at me with some motive in their eyes. And I liked being a big brother."

"You're still my big brother," Omolewa said. "And as for motives, how do you know I didn't have any?"

"Because you are too honest," he said. "Be wary of that. Don't forget what looms in the shadows."

Kulal's warning sobered her mood.

"Is she coming?" Omolewa asked.

"No. Mama is not one for emotional goodbyes. She wishes you well. She also sent you a gift."

Omolewa sighed. "She's already given us enough. We left Nacala as paupers and we'll return as rich folk. We need nothing else."

"You will need this," Kulal said.

He motioned his head toward the dock. A wagon had arrived, filled with sturdy wooden chests.

"What's inside those chests?" Omolewa asked.

"Kashta's books," Kulal replied. "He brought them to the Dry Season Palace. He intended to teach you from these volumes. And these are no ordinary books. They're tomes from Kamit. I suspect Kashta's elders would not be very happy with him if they knew he planned to share this knowledge with you. The Kamites are jealous with their secrets."

"I don't know," Omolewa said. "I'm not sure I can understand them without his guidance."

"You'll be fine," he said. "You're smarter than most. You'll figure it out."

"You should send them back," she insisted. "I feel like I'm stealing from the dead."

"Too late for that," Kulal said.

Drums rumbling like a monsoon storm interrupted them. Omolewa and Kulal looked toward the palace, Kulal with an amused look on his face.

"She said wasn't coming," he said. "I guess she changed her mind."

Omolewa tensed. The last thing she wanted was a confrontation with the Bene. She took a deep breath then proceeded to the dock. On the way baba and mama joined her, Diwani and Kazija trailing behind. They waited as the royal procession made its way through the city, Zimbabwans stepping aside and prostrating as columns of warriors preceding the carriage marched by. The warriors formed an armed corridor to the docks, their faces stern as the Bene's bodyguards opened the carriage door. The Bene emerged, resplendent in a wrapped dress of shimmering gold fabric and headwrap. Omolewa and her parents prostrated as she approached, Omolewa trying to keep her hands from shaking.

"Please rise," the Bene said.

Omolewa came to her feet standing before the Bene. Her true mother's regal countenance faded away, replaced by a melancholy smile. She wrapped her arms around Omolewa, hugging her tight. Omolewa's hug was not as generous.

The Bene pulled away.

"I do wish you well, Omolewa," she said. "I had hoped things would be different, but Eda knows better than us all. Be mindful of your abilities and do not draw attention to yourself. Remember the coming storm."

"I will," Omolewa said. "Thank you for everything you've done and everything you tried to do. I'm sorry I didn't turn out to be the daughter you wanted me to be."

"On the contrary. You are more than I imagined. Much more."

The Bene bent forward then kissed her cheek.

"I love you," she whispered.

Omolewa wanted to answer the same, but to do so would be a lie. Instead, she hugged the Bene.

"I expect you to keep your promise to me, Mikijen," the Bene said to baba. "Keep my daughter safe."

Baba stood beside Omolewa then hugged her.

"I will," he said.

The Bene then looked at mama.

"You did well raising her. Thank you."

Mama nodded then smiled.

The Bene's regal demeanor returned.

"Come Kulal," she said. "It is time we returned to our duties."

Kulal rushed toward Omolewa, lifting her off her feet then spinning her around. They both laughed.

"Goodbye, sister," he said. "If you don't learn anything else, learn to be a better thief."

Omolewa kissed his cheek.

"I will."

Kulal set her down then followed the Bene to the carriage. Omolewa and her family waited for the procession to begin the journey back to the Central Palace before boarding the dhow once again. It took the nahoda and his crew another hour to secure the dhow and its cargo before the anchor was lifted and the mooring ropes untied. Omolewa and her family stood together at the stern, taking one more look at their adopted home. As her family waved at the crowd that came to see them off, Omolewa wandered to the bow. She looked toward the horizon. Pik-Pik emerged from her pouch and Omolewa held her in her hands, stroking her soft fur.

"Time to go home," she whispered.

The monsoon winds filled the sails, pushing Omolewa back to a familiar place and a new future.

-End-

ABOUT THE AUTHOR

Milton Davis is a Black Fantastic fiction author and owner of MVmedia, LLC, a publishing company specializing in Science Fiction, Fantasy based on African/African Diaspora culture, history, and traditions. Milton is the author of twenty-one books and publisher/editor of ten anthologies. His stories *The Swarm* (2017) and *Carnival* (2020) were nominated the for the British Science Fiction Award. His story, *The Monsters of Mena Ngai* appears in the Black Panther: Tales of Wakanda anthology.

We hope you enjoyed The Bene's Daughter. Check out our other middle grade/young adult titles at www.mvmediaatl.com and anywhere books are sold.

Thirteen-year-old Amber Robinson's life is full of changes. Her parents are sending her to a private school away from her friends, and high school looms before her. But little does she know that her biggest change awaits in a mysterious city hidden from the world for a thousand years.

Prepare yourself for an exciting adventure that spans from the Atlanta suburbs to the grasslands of Mali. It's a story of a girl who discovers her hidden abilities and heritage in a way that surprises and entertains.

Clifton Academy is everything Amber thought it would be... and worse. In addition to trying to fit in at a new school, she struggles to master her newfound talents. One day she is contacted by Grandma Alake and is told she must once again defend Marai from the sorcerer Bagule and his companion, Nieleni. The nefarious duo is in search of Sonni Ali's sword, a talisman so powerful possessing could mean the end of the ancient and secret city. Can Amber and her friends find the sword before Bagule and save Marai once more?

The year: 1920
When famed magician, Dr. Marvellus Djinn, selects a motley crew of talented teens to tour her theme park of magic and mythological creatures, all are elated for the opportunity. Once they arrive, the odd scholars realize Dr. Djinn is more than just a wealthy magician eager to provide Colored folks with an escape from Jim Crow. From cotton candy teleportation to haunted obelisks and swallowing monsters, The Motherland packs a thrilling, and dangerous, punch.

www.ingramcontent.com/pod-product-compliance
Lightning Source LLC
Chambersburg PA
CBHW051655260626
47170CB00004B/1510